Maisie Frobisher

Gone to Ground

Liz Hedgecock

WHITE
RHINO
BOOKS

Copyright © Liz Hedgecock, 2020

All rights reserved. Apart from any use permitted under UK copyright law, no part of this publication may be reproduced, stored in a retrieval system, or transmitted, in any form or by any means, electronic, mechanical, photocopying, recording or otherwise, without the prior written permission of the copyright owner.

This is a work of fiction. Names, characters, businesses, places, events and incidents are either the products of the author's imagination or used in a fictitious manner. Any resemblance to actual persons, living or dead, or actual events is purely coincidental.

ISBN-13: 979-8638054762

*For Virginia Hall (1906-1982)
ambulance driver, wireless operator, and
secret agent*

CHAPTER 1

'Tomorrow?'

'Yes, tomorrow.' Another waltzing couple whirled towards them, but Inspector Hamilton executed a reverse turn in the nick of time and steered Maisie safely away.

Maisie did not have breath to speak for some time; and so many couples filled the room that she worried about their being overheard. Perhaps, soon, that would be at an end.

Her life had been a whirl since their arrival in Calcutta, yet at the same time, curiously dull. It was not that she had nothing to do; rather that it was a social round of tea parties and entertainments and picnics and introductions which required little but pleasantries. Inspector Hamilton — Fraser, as Maisie supposed she should get used to calling him — had been subjected to the same treatment, and Maisie could see in the tension of his shoulders and the slight restlessness he had begun to exhibit that it was doing him no good. Tonight's dance had helped to release some of that tension, but she had not expected what followed.

'Let's return to England,' he had whispered in her ear, a few dances in. 'We can catch the mail train to Bombay on Saturday. I'll explain to Lord Montgomery, and ask for an extended leave of absence. And if he won't grant that leave, well, I'll go back to my old job in London.'

Maisie realised she was gripping the inspector somewhat harder than the dance required, and loosened her hold on him a little. 'Are you sure?'

'Yes,' he said. 'The viceroy doesn't have anything for me, and I would be much better employed at home. Besides, I want to pay a call on your parents, and more particularly your father.'

Maisie's heart leapt. Fraser's proposal had hung in the air for a few days. First she had waited for him to mention it. When he did not, she had worried that perhaps he had only half-meant it, or saw it far in the future, and so she had not mentioned it either.

'You mean…?'

'Yes, I do. I can hardly carry you off without a word to your family, can I? And of course my family will want to meet you.'

'Will they?'

He laughed. 'Of course they will! I am the baby of the family, don't forget, and they will want to be sure that you are not a designing woman.'

'And what if I am?' whispered Maisie.

'Then they'll have to put up with it,' Inspector Hamilton replied, just as the dance came to an end.

There is so much to do, thought Maisie, as Fraser escorted her to the buffet. A dress to have made — though in Bombay she could always ask Mrs Beaumont to run up one of her specials. There would be the wedding breakfast to organise — but would her mother do that? Or would that be Fraser's mother's responsibility? She shivered at the idea of someone she had never met, or even seen, deciding what food she would eat at her own wedding. Although of course Fraser's mother would be very nice. Or she hoped she would. Then what about his father, and brothers? And wasn't there a sister? Suddenly Fraser seemed to have the best of the bargain, since he only had to meet her parents. And they were both dears, obviously.

'It will be so nice to be able to be alone together again,' she said. 'Do you remember those sunrises on the *Britannia*?'

'Not particularly,' he said, and Maisie raised her eyebrows at him. Then he smiled. 'I was too busy looking at you most of the time.'

'Oh, really,' she said. 'I suppose that is rather romantic, and I ought to appreciate it.'

'Yes, you ought,' he replied, 'for I seldom make pretty speeches, so you had best appreciate the ones you get.' He found Maisie a seat, and brought her a plate of food. 'Will you mind leaving Calcutta so soon?'

'I should like to have seen a little more of it, perhaps,' said Maisie. 'Although I think I have done all the sights. As have you.'

'To the detriment of my shoe leather,' said the inspector. 'I may have to buy a new pair in Bombay, in preparation for the promenades we shall make on board ship.'

'I am looking forward to doing absolutely nothing,' said Maisie. 'No wild-goose chases, no escapades —'

'No fancy-dress balls?' asked the inspector. He grinned, and his sudden transformation from stern to mischievous reminded Maisie of the first time he had smiled at her properly, not so very long ago.

She grinned back. 'Perhaps one or two.' She thought for a moment. 'I suppose I had better say nothing to Ruth until it is official and we have our tickets.'

'I'm not sure she'll approve,' said the inspector. 'After all, she has just got here.'

'Yes, and she only unpacked yesterday. Oh dear.' Maisie reflected that Ruth would probably think her even more unreasonable than usual. But Ruth had not been through the adventures that she had. And hopefully she would never find out the half of it. 'I shall definitely hold my tongue, then.'

'And you had better do so now,' said Inspector Hamilton. 'Captain James is approaching, and I have a distinct feeling that he will lecture me for dancing so much with you, and entreat me to favour the other ladies.'

'What it is to be in demand,' said Maisie lightly. Eyeing Captain James, she judged that the inspector was probably right. He did have, underneath his charming smile, a determined look on his face.

'It will be over soon,' she said. 'You may dance with

your other ladies, and I shall test out some other men, and then you can tell the viceroy in the morning.'

'Hamilton, would you do me the honour of a word?' asked Captain James. Maisie decided that another crayfish sandwich was just what she needed, and moved discreetly away.

***

Any fears that Maisie might have had of being a wallflower for the rest of the evening were soon allayed. Captain James approached her within ten minutes, accompanied by a nervous young man. 'Miss Frobisher, allow me to introduce Mr Frederick Aitchison, attaché to the Crown Prince of Raponia. Mr Aitchison, this is Miss Frobisher, who has just joined us from Bombay.'

'Delighted,' murmured Maisie, half-curtsying to the young man, who blushed.

'Oh, yes, delighted,' the young man replied, with an unexpectedly low bow. 'Um, would you like to dance?'

Maisie listened to the music, which currently was a reasonably staid waltz. 'Yes, that would be lovely,' she replied. *It will help take my mind off things*, she thought.

Certainly for the first half of the dance she achieved that; for Mr Aitchison was rather awkward, and it took most of Maisie's concentration and diplomacy to steer him round without making it look as if she were leading. However, as he relaxed his dancing improved, and soon Maisie had leisure to gaze about her. Of course almost the first person she saw was Fraser Hamilton, sweeping a young lady round the floor whose blushes rivalled her bright pink gown. He grinned at her over the young woman's shoulder, and with another turn he was gone.

How do I feel about returning to England? In some ways the thought of coming back in a sort of triumph, with a handsome man on one's arm, was attractive; but then again — *Magnificently independent and free of men,* she thought. 'That was what I said, wasn't it?'

'I beg your pardon?' asked Mr Aitchison.

'I'm so sorry,' said Maisie. 'I was thinking of a letter I wrote this morning.'

'Oh I see,' he said. 'I sometimes do that. Remember something I wrote, and wonder if I could have put it better. You know, with more of a flourish.'

'Exactly,' said Maisie. *I left England with a flourish to travel the world, and returning to marry and settle down is not exactly what I had in mind. Of course, it is nothing like that really,* she added hastily to herself.

But people will think it is, a little voice whispered, so clearly that Maisie looked around to see who was speaking. 'Never mind people,' she said crossly.

'No, indeed,' Mr Aitchison agreed. Maisie clamped her mouth shut and resolved to speak and think no more until the dance was over. At that point Captain James strolled across with another gentleman for Maisie to take round the floor, to an energetic polka which taxed her energy sufficiently to keep her from thinking too deeply. For that she was grateful, though conscious that somehow she had become part of the viceroy's establishment, in that she was required to do her duty in terms of dancing with newcomers. *I am part of the furniture*, she thought, and that notion was rather uncomfortable.

Fraser claimed her for the last dance of the evening. 'I see you have been busy,' he murmured in her ear. 'Were the young men you tested to your liking?'

'Oh absolutely,' replied Maisie. 'They keep one's feet busy, if not one's brain.'

He laughed. 'Well, for my part I have been blushed at, giggled at, and had my foot stepped on once or twice.'

'At least I never did that to you,' said Maisie. 'Are you still resolved to tell the viceroy tomorrow?'

'Oh yes.' He looked down at her. 'Why, are you having second thoughts?'

'No, not at all,' said Maisie, 'but —'

'But what?' Fraser had a puzzled expression on his face. Maisie realised that they had stopped dancing, and tapped his arm before people crashed into them.

'I was thinking... It would be nice to return to Bombay, and spend a little time there first,' she said. 'I never did get to enjoy my triumph in Bombay society. I have had charming letters from the Darlings, and it would be most satisfactory to watch them eat humble pie in person, after their desertion of me in my time of need. And we could call on the Merritts, and discover how married life is suiting them.'

'That's true,' said Fraser. 'Perhaps Christopher Merritt will tell me such hair-raising tales of married life that I shall go off the idea entirely.'

'Perhaps,' said Maisie. 'It would be a terrible shame to go all the way back to England only to discover that we couldn't stand each other.'

'Precisely,' said Fraser, and squeezed her hand.

They teased each other in the same vein on the carriage ride to Maisie's hotel. Maisie was glad; it saved her from thinking too deeply about the matter. But once Ruth had made her ready for bed, and Maisie was alone in the dark, quiet room, possibilities raced through her mind. Did it matter what people thought? Could she, somehow, live the same sort of life in England as she had since embarking on the *SS Britannia*? *I can't know until I try*, she thought, *but at least I have a stay of execution.* That word made her pause. *Execution.* Was that what her return to England might be? Cutting off this new life before it had really begun? 'Please, no,' whispered Maisie, squeezing her eyes tight shut. It would be lovely to see her parents again, and her friends, but — not at that price. *I shall see what tomorrow brings*, she told herself firmly; but the words brought her no peace at all.

CHAPTER 2

'Which dress, Miss Maisie?' asked Ruth.

Maisie considered. 'The lilac, please.'

Ruth's eyebrows climbed up her forehead. 'Are we going somewhere nice today? I didn't know you had an engagement.'

Maisie stared at her maid before realising that Ruth meant the word in its normal sense. 'Not exactly; the inspector said he might call sometime this morning.'

Ruth's eyebrows climbed a little higher. 'Inspector Hamilton? But wasn't he at the ball last night?'

'He was,' said Maisie, keeping her tone as light as she could.

'I thought so,' said Ruth, smoothing the folds of the lilac dress. 'Is he going to settle in Calcutta?'

'I'm not sure,' said Maisie. 'I don't think he knows himself.' She felt a pang at not being able to confide in

Ruth; that seemed to be happening more and more lately, and it was not a development she welcomed. 'What do you think of Calcutta, Ruth?'

'I'll tell you when I've had a chance to see it, Miss Maisie,' Ruth retorted, laying out the dress and going to the chest of drawers for gloves and a fan. 'Since I've arrived I've done very little but put your things in order and run errands.' Maisie stole a glance at her, but Ruth looked cheerful rather than annoyed.

'Well, you didn't like the idea of twiddling your thumbs in Bombay,' she remarked.

'That I didn't,' Ruth replied. 'At least there's a bit more go to this place, what with the viceroy and all. Now, let's get you into this dress before the inspector comes.'

She was fastening the last button on Maisie's bodice when a tap at the door made them both gasp. 'In the nick of time,' said Ruth, handing Maisie her gloves. 'Do give the inspector my regards.' She winked at Maisie, and before she could reply, whisked from the room.

***

'What do you mean, no?'

When the page had announced her visitor, Maisie's heart had leapt with joy. Then she had gone down to the veranda, and seen the inspector's face.

'Exactly that,' he snapped. 'Apparently I can't be let go. There is too much to do here. I ventured to remark that apart from clearing up the Howarth business I haven't seen much of it, and he said "That's just the beginning."'

'Did you explain why you wished to leave?' asked Maisie, her heart sinking.

'I did. And he's not keen on that idea, either.'

'Oh.' Maisie sat down abruptly. The plans she had been building in her head tumbled around her ears, and she rubbed her forehead as if they had made a physical sound. 'Did he say what he wants you to do?'

'Delve deeper,' said the inspector. His stern face had definitely returned. 'Find out who and what is behind Leopard. See what I can learn about Saunders.' A short, quick huff. 'Although why it takes me to do that —'

'It doesn't, does it?' said Maisie. A surge of anger, and with it energy, welled up inside her. 'I shall go and see him. He's got a mansion full of staff; he doesn't need you too.'

The inspector looked a little hurt, and also taken aback. 'Perhaps he appreciates my skills,' he replied.

'I didn't mean — oh, you know what I mean!' cried Maisie. 'I need you more than he does.'

'Really?' The inspector smiled.

Maisie sighed. 'Yes, really.'

He sat in the chair beside her, and took her hand. 'I suppose I ought to thank you for that — should I say compliment?'

Maisie opened her mouth to say that it wasn't a compliment exactly, and changed her mind as he leaned towards her. His lips brushed hers, and the waiter cleared his throat loudly.

'Come along,' said the inspector. 'Lord Strathcairn has given me an hour to break the news to you, and then he wants me back at the office. And he has an appointment at eleven. So if you are going to give him a piece of your mind, we had better be quick.'

***

At Government House they were shown into the room where they had waited, with the Carters and Mr Howarth, only a matter of days ago. *At least I am better dressed this time*, thought Maisie, catching sight of herself in the mirror over the mantelpiece.

They sat together, on the same settee. Maisie had entered the room full of righteous indignation; but as they waited, and the hands of the clock ticked round, she could feel it dissipating, as if it were being leached out of her by the horsehair sofa, the carved wood furnishings, and the formal photographs which ornamented the room.

It was twenty minutes to eleven when a brisk tap at the door was followed by the viceroy himself. Maisie was so used to seeing him in full evening dress, officiating at one of his functions, that his linen suit took her by surprise. 'Good morning,' she gabbled, rising to her feet.

'Oh, do sit down, the pair of you,' Lord Strathcairn said testily. 'I suppose you want to be off sightseeing, Miss Frobisher, and you have come to tell me to give you your inspector back.'

Maisie gasped. 'Hardly that, Your Excellency, but —'

'That's the gist of it, though, isn't it?' The viceroy smiled in a resigned way. 'I'm sorry, Miss Frobisher, but it can't be helped. I need Hamilton here, and that's the end of it.'

'But why?' Maisie felt light pressure on the hand Fraser was holding, and interpreted it as a warning. 'I would be most grateful if you could explain it to me, Your

Excellency.'

'Very prettily spoken, Miss Frobisher,' said the viceroy. 'Then I shall. I dare say that Hamilton has given you a précis of our earlier conversation. Haven't you?'

Fraser started slightly. 'Yes, Your Excellency, I have.'

'Good. Saves time. So I gather you both thought matters were done and dusted. You've bagged Howarth and brought him in, and he's told us what he knows. Therefore he can be dealt with appropriately while you return to England as conquering heroes.'

'That wasn't quite —'

'Well, you may not.' The viceroy looked at them both keenly. 'Excuse me for interrupting you, but we haven't much time. The fact is that, though I'm pretty sure Howarth has made a clean breast of everything he knows, that's less than half the story. And I need the full story to be able to act.'

'F — Inspector Hamilton said that you wanted him to find out who is behind Leopard,' said Maisie faintly.

'That's right,' said Lord Strathcairn. 'But there's more. I've been in communication with Montgomery at Bombay and he's pulled out every instance of trouble in the last three years that could possibly stem from leaked information. I also sent a trusted man to go through as much of the relevant paperwork at the secretariat as he could. The likelihood, as you may already have guessed, is that Howarth's contribution to this mess is somewhat less impressive than he thinks.'

'So there is someone else?' asked Maisie.

'It appears so,' said the viceroy. 'And I'm pretty sure,

given the wealth of information which Howarth has furnished us with already, that if he knew, he'd have told us.'

'But in that case,' Fraser said slowly, 'wouldn't it make sense for me to return to the secretariat —'

'It would, if I didn't think that whoever it is in Bombay is already wise to the fact that you are no more a Civil Service man than Miss Frobisher here.' The viceroy smiled. 'I've told Montgomery to keep my man for now as a replacement for Howarth, who is "engaged on important work for me for the next few months", and I can trust him to keep his eyes and ears open.'

'So what shall I be doing?' asked Fraser. Maisie heard the frustration in his voice, and squeezed his hand in turn.

'Leopard, or Anton De Souza, to give him his proper name, is our key,' said Lord Strathcairn. 'You've settled in well, Hamilton, so I'd like you to move into Government House and make De Souza your full-time job. That, and finding out more about Saunders. His movements while he was on furlough, before he came back to India and recruited Howarth; the people he befriended at Simla; any letters he had, any papers he left. If we can find a link between Saunders and Leopard, or whoever was above him, we are in a fair way to make real progress.'

'And what about me?' said Maisie, in a voice that sounded very small and young to herself.

'Oh, I'm sure you can help, Miss Frobisher,' said the viceroy. 'There will be plenty of documents, and it would be best if we had a dedicated and secure room for the information. You could set that up and organise it, I'm sure.' He smiled at Maisie, and rose to his feet. 'If that's all —'

'Don't you have a clerk who can do that?'

The viceroy looked as surprised as if the clock had spoken. 'I beg your pardon, Miss Frobisher?'

Maisie glared at him. 'I said, Your Excellency, that given the number of staff you have, surely you can spare one of them to do this — office work.'

The viceroy raised his eyebrows. 'I thought you two would want to work together.'

'I didn't come to India to work in an office,' said Maisie. 'I'm sorry, Your Excellency, but my answer is no.'

The viceroy's eyes rested on her thoughtfully, and Maisie tried not to wriggle. 'I see,' he said. 'Perhaps I should give you a little more information. Do you remember the reception you attended when you first arrived?'

Maisie nodded.

'Good. And do you remember the group of Indians who muttered amongst themselves when I talked about representation and working together?'

Maisie swallowed, and nodded again.

'Excellent. You probably think I shall tell you that they are the problem. Well, they are not. My personal view is that one day India will rule herself — not yet, but perhaps in the new century. Personally, I don't mind that idea one bit.'

He paused. 'However, as Viceroy of India I am serving not just this country, but the Empress of India herself, and I doubt she is willing to give up this part of her empire. On one hand I have Indian dignitaries telling me that they prefer the old style of civil servant because they knew where they were with them, and on the other I have people within the Service who write newspaper articles about their nationalist sympathies, and how things ought to be.'

Lord Strathcairn let out a long sigh, and for the first time Maisie noticed how tired he appeared, even at this time of day. 'Somehow I must keep this vast, complicated mess in some sort of order. The last thing I need is idiots like Howarth stirring up trouble for money, and behind them, people trying to bring the country down about our ears.'

Maisie opened her mouth, then closed it, for want of anything to say.

'Have I shocked you?' The viceroy smiled. 'Forgive me for speaking so frankly, Miss Frobisher, but I suspected that if you could see the bigger picture, it might change your answer.'

'May I — may I think the matter over?' asked Maisie.

The viceroy gazed at her with incurious eyes. 'You may.' He rose. 'As you say, doubtless somewhere in my staff I have a lowly clerk who could carry out the tasks I suggested; but you would bring something to the role which he could not.' He bowed.

'I shall think it over —' Maisie began; but the door was already closing behind Lord Strathcairn.

She looked up at Fraser. 'Well, you said your piece,' he said.

'Yes, and I wasn't beheaded,' Maisie replied, though in truth she felt as if she had passed through a mangle.

'I'd better go,' said the inspector. 'Things to do, documents to read.' He bent and kissed Maisie. 'Dinner this evening? I'll wire you at the hotel if I can make it.'

'Yes, that would be lovely,' said Maisie automatically.

Fraser left, and she climbed into a rickshaw to return to her hotel. Calcutta was at its brightest; but Maisie had no eyes for her surroundings. Somehow she had managed to get herself into a position where nothing was what she wanted, and every choice was wrong. She sighed, and watched a fruit-seller juggling mangoes, to the delight of several small children. 'Why can't life be simple?' she said aloud, and resigned herself to a day of indecision, speculation, and worry.

CHAPTER 3

Maisie arrived back at her hotel suite to find Ruth sitting in her armchair and frowning at a stocking heel. Ruth glanced up as the door opened and, holding the stocking carefully, jumped to her feet. 'I thought I would get on with some mending, Miss Maisie, while you were gone —'

'Just in case I had anything to tell you when I returned?' Maisie motioned to Ruth to sit down again.

'I take it that it isn't good news, Miss Maisie,' said Ruth, laying the stocking aside and folding her hands in her lap as if expecting a tale.

'Not really, no,' said Maisie, unpinning her hat and sitting in the other armchair, heedless of creases.

Distress fluttered over Ruth's face for a moment, but passed quickly. 'Is it — is it anything I ought to know about, Miss Maisie?'

'Is that your business, Ruth?' Ruth looked hurt at that,

and Maisie regretted it instantly. 'I'm sorry. I'm a bit — confused. Inspector Hamilton asked the viceroy for leave to go, and the viceroy has refused.'

'But what does that have to do with us — I mean you?'

'Everything,' said Maisie, and put her face in her hands. She did not feel like crying, but she wished to hide her face from Ruth's scrutiny.

'But I thought you liked Inspector Hamilton,' said Ruth.

'I do!' cried Maisie. 'That's the problem. He has asked me to marry him, and wants to return to England, and I didn't know how I felt about that, so I suggested Bombay, but now the viceroy wants *me* to work for him too, and — and I don't know what to do!' The tears came, and presently she felt a wiry but comforting arm around her shoulders, and a handkerchief pressed into her hand.

'I'll order tea,' murmured Ruth, 'and the post came while you were away. I have left it on the dressing table for you.' The door closed quietly, and Maisie was alone.

It was easier to pull herself together in the knowledge that she wasn't being watched by a sympathetic eye. Soon Maisie was able to dry her eyes and look around her without the world being a blur. The prospect of letters lifted her spirits. Who had written? She sat down at the dressing table, more careful of her skirts this time, picked up her silver letter opener, and slit the first envelope, which was addressed in a hand she vaguely knew.

Dearest Maisie,
Please would you consider coming back to Bombay?

Nora, Mary and I are half distracted, and the place is so quiet without you. Even Captain Hanson seems disconsolate.

If you return, I'm sure they would hold a ball in your honour. It is rather dead here, and more so now that the Smythes have departed — for Sweden, of all places. The governor hosted a little farewell dinner for them — nothing much, just thirty or so — and Mrs Smythe looked as if she were drinking sour cream, not champagne!

If my entreaty is not strong enough to bring you back, please consider Edward Mandeville. He is pining, poor young man — even his moustache is drooping — although I'm not sure whether that is for love of you, or oppression by his new taskmaster, whom he says is a Tartar.

All my love,
Julia (Darling)

Maisie's mouth twisted, half in amusement, half distaste. She opened the second envelope, addressed in Connie's familiar hand, to take the taste away.

Dear Maisie,

I do hope that my letters are reaching you, after all the mix-ups with the post while you were on board ship. I hope that you are enjoying Bombay, and that the people are more congenial than your shipmates were.

Life is much the same as usual here. Bee is eating like a horse and growing like a weed, while Albert merely eats like a horse. I think Mrs Jones considers the empty plates a compliment to her cooking; but in truth those two would eat almost anything. Katherine and I are between cases at present, but I suspect that will not last long.

Will you return home for Christmas, or will you spend it in India? If you do, please write and tell us about it, for I can't imagine Christmas in a warm place.

Much love,
Connie

'Oh dear,' murmured Maisie. 'I must wire and tell Connie my new address. Unless —' She pushed a stray curl off her face. 'I am so behind with my correspondence,' she whispered. Connie's letter made her feel guilty, so she put it under Julia's, and turned to the next.

Dear Maisie,

I'm not sure if it is proper to call you Maisie, but the Darlings do, and I have fallen into the habit of it.

I hope you are well, and enjoying Calcutta. We all miss you, and now that Howarth has gone on to higher things I almost miss him too. Our new man, Hailey, is a martinet — and I thought Howarth was strict! We do not see too much of Hailey; for he shuts himself up in a little room and only comes out to give orders and check our work. I must admit that the work is much more interesting, and the time passes more quickly. I think Hailey was rather shocked at what Howarth had me doing; he asked lots of questions about that. I don't know whether he really thinks Howarth was a slacker, or whether he is just trying to make himself look good. I suppose time will tell when he settles down.

Do come back soon, Maisie, or we shall miss each other completely. Hailey has given me a small district to administer, and he says I shall spend most of my time out of the secretariat for the next few months. I daresay I shall be riding all over the province, holding court under trees, and speaking every language save my own when that happens. A visit from you beforehand would buck me up and enable me to face the ordeal.

Yours ever,
Edward Mandeville

Maisie smiled as she refolded the letter. She tried to imagine Edward Mandeville settling disputes and dispensing justice, and with a giggle, turned to the next letter.

Dear Miss Frobisher,

Sending you a line to ask privately what the position is with the viceroy. I expected you and Hamilton back by return, but Hamilton can't give me a straight answer, and all I get from Strathcairn is requests for more information.

Speaking of which, any information from you is most welcome. Hope you're well and your gun is idle.

Regards,
Montgomery

'Miss Frobisher,' Ruth called faintly, 'I have a tea tray.'

Maisie sprang up and opened the door. 'I said I'd bring it myself to save trouble,' said Ruth, setting the tray on the nearest table. 'They are so respectful that I feel guilty.'

'I shall order you to pour out then, Ruth, once it is brewed,' said Maisie with a smile.

'I'm glad you're feeling brighter, Miss Maisie,' said Ruth, taking the lid off the teapot and stirring the leaves. 'Any interesting letters?'

'Apparently all of Bombay misses me,' said Maisie.

'I'm sure they do,' said Ruth, 'but to be honest I would rather remain in Calcutta for a while. The train didn't agree with me.'

'Oh, I'm sorry,' said Maisie. 'Were you train-sick?'

'Not exactly,' said Ruth, 'I did feel wobbly when I tried to go anywhere, though. I got out at every stop and had a little walk on the platform to right myself, but within half an hour I felt just the same. And my neighbour on the train was an odd lady indeed.'

Maisie laughed. 'What was she like?'

Ruth poured them both a cup of tea before answering, and Maisie suspected it was to consider her answer. 'Well, the rest of us in the servants' carriage were, naturally, servants, for we compared notes — Of course I said that you were a very considerate mistress.'

'Of course,' agreed Maisie. 'So she wasn't a servant?'

Ruth shrugged. 'I don't think she could have been, for she was dressed in such an odd combination of clothing — all British-looking, but nothing matched. Her dress was quite nice, but her hat was battered and faded. If you had told me she had stolen her outfit from a washing line, I wouldn't have been surprised.'

'Perhaps she did,' said Maisie. 'What else was odd about her, apart from her outfit?'

'She was so *red*,' said Ruth. 'She must have suffered a bad sunburn, for her face was pink and puffy, but her hair was bright red too, a sort of copper. It clashed with her face, to be honest.'

'The poor woman!' exclaimed Maisie. 'Hopefully her sunburn will fade, and then she will not clash with herself. Was she odd in manner too?'

'Not particularly,' said Ruth. 'She was very quiet apart from her cough. She said she was going to Calcutta to visit a friend, and that was all she did say.' Ruth sipped her tea, looking as if she could divine things from its depths. 'Anyway…' She set her cup down. 'Have you decided what to do about the inspector?'

'If he is staying,' said Maisie, 'I shall stay too. I would love to return to Bombay, but I suppose it can wait. We are both needed here.' A thought struck her, and she glanced up at Ruth. 'When I said earlier that the inspector had asked me to marry him, you never said a word!'

'It was hardly unexpected,' said Ruth, smiling. 'Anyone with eyes can see you two are a match.'

Maisie laughed. 'I'm glad you approve, Ruth.' She sipped her own tea and set the cup down decisively. 'I shall write to my Bombay correspondents to inform them that I shall not be returning just yet, and wire Connie with my new address.' She paused. 'Would you mind pressing this dress, Ruth? I should like to wear it this evening for dinner with the inspector.'

Ruth heaved a dramatic sigh, then grinned. 'Very well, Miss Frobisher.' She waited while Maisie changed into a tea gown, then departed with her bundle of lilac airiness.

Maisie dashed off the letters without too much thought, since really they were but polite refusals — what could she say about her current situation that was not a falsehood? Her hand moved towards the bell, then stopped. *I shall take them myself, and stretch my legs.*

The concierge started as she approached. 'Miss Frobisher, I thought that you had gone out for the day.'

'No, I just paid a call this morning,' said Maisie. 'I have been in my room writing letters for the last hour or so.'

'What a pity,' said the concierge, a look of genuine regret crossing his face. 'Someone came to the desk and asked for you.'

'Oh, who? Was it Inspector Hamilton?'

'No, it was a — an Englishwoman. She asked for you by name, and described you. I thought she must know you, so I said that you were out and offered to take a message, but she would not leave any.'

'How peculiar,' said Maisie. She frowned. A lady — no, the concierge had not said *lady*. He had said *Englishwoman*. *A woman, not a lady, who knows me, but will not leave a message.* 'If she returns, ask her to leave her name at least, for I'm sure I don't know who it can be.'

'Yes, ma'am,' said the concierge.

Maisie gave him her letters and her wire, with payment and instructions, and turned to go. A thought struck her. 'If you don't mind me asking, what colour was her hair?'

'How odd that you should ask!' exclaimed the concierge. 'It was red — bright red.'

CHAPTER 4

'Another box?' Maisie stared in dismay as Mr Finnemore, the clerk assigned to them, carried in another tea chest.

'I'm afraid so, madam.' Mr Finnemore set the box down on the floor — for there was no other unoccupied flat surface in the room. He pulled out a large handkerchief and mopped his brow. 'Believe me, Miss Frobisher, I shall be as glad as you when all the papers are transported. We are almost there.'

'Oh good!' exclaimed Maisie.

'Yes, indeed,' said Mr Finnemore. 'I believe Hailey is sending more papers by the next Bombay mail, and then hopefully we shall have everything gathered together.' He smiled with the weary satisfaction of a bureaucrat engaged in a momentous, yet tedious task that must be done. 'Will you require anything else, madam? Inspector?'

'I suppose a box of matches is too much to ask,' said

Fraser from the window, where he was watching Calcutta go about its business.

'Ha ha, very good, sir,' said Mr Finnemore. He took out a large pocket watch and glanced at it. 'I see it is almost eleven o'clock, so the tea trolley will doubtless appear shortly. I am sure that will be a great help.' He bowed, and withdrew.

'I am not sure that all the tea in India could help with this,' said Maisie, gazing at the piles of paper and boxes in despair.

'Well, we must get on and do our best, I suppose,' said Fraser. He removed the lid of the tea chest which Mr Finnemore had brought, gazed at the jumble of papers within, said something which, perhaps fortunately, was inaudible, and replaced the lid.

'That won't help,' said Maisie decisively, walking to the desk and removing another lid. 'At least if we can work out what is in each box we can sort them into categories.' She counted on her fingers. 'Papers from Bombay that Howarth has tampered with or which concern him; papers from there which, as far as we know, he has had no hand in; information about Saunders; and information about Leopard.'

'Very succinct,' said Inspector Hamilton. 'I am beginning to think you have more of a natural aptitude for this work than I do.'

'Please don't tell anybody that,' said Maisie. She pulled out a bundle of papers, and with them a small cloud of dust. 'Ugh!' she cried, and sneezed. Luckily a knock at the door heralded the promised tea trolley, allowing her to put off further excavation of the box for another ten minutes or so.

It had sounded rather romantic the night before. Fraser had found an intimate little restaurant on the Chowringhee Road, and over kosha mangsho and mint tea they had seemed great adventurers, delving into the past and solving mysteries which had gone unsolved — nay, unnoticed — for years. 'With us both working on it,' Fraser had said, 'it will only take half as long. Who knows, we may find a clue tomorrow which will set us on the right track, and then we can make haste to Bombay with clear consciences.'

'Indeed we can,' said Maisie. Fraser slid his hand across the tablecloth, and she took it.

But now, looking over the rim of a cup of tea at boxes and boxes of documents, and with the day getting warmer, Maisie felt merely despondent. 'Come on,' she said, setting down her cup. 'The sooner we begin, the sooner we may find something.' She picked up the papers, and holding them at arm's-length, shook them thoroughly to remove the dust. 'I might ask Ruth to lend me an apron,' she said, wrinkling her nose.

They worked for perhaps twenty minutes, the quiet punctuated only by an occasional sigh from Maisie, or a grunt from the inspector. The first box was done, and the papers filed in piles on the floor according to Maisie's classification. 'Once we have cleared the desk,' she said, 'we can move the piles to there, or perhaps use the empty tea chests, until we get a filing cabinet.'

Fraser snorted, without looking up from his document.

A smart knock at the door, and a cry of 'Good

morning!' in a female voice sent Maisie hurrying to open the door.

'Mrs Carter!' she cried, smiling. 'How lovely to see you! I don't suppose you have come to help us with our paper-sorting?'

'Certainly not,' said Mrs Carter, sweeping in and knocking over one of Maisie's piles with her skirt. 'Paperwork is the bane of my existence and I avoid it wherever possible. I heard about your, um, undertaking, and came to see how you were getting on.'

'We have begun,' said Maisie. 'I won't shake your hand, because I am quite dusty.'

'Likewise,' said Inspector Hamilton, bowing.

'I can see you are,' said Mrs Carter, her nose wrinkling slightly. 'Here.' She opened her bag and handed Maisie and the inspector two pairs of white cotton gloves. 'Not so much for the dirt as the paper cuts.'

'Thank you for your assistance,' said Fraser, drawing the gloves on. 'Are you engaged in anything at present?'

'Oh no,' said Mrs Carter. 'It is Randolph who is working, not I.' The way that she said it, however, made Maisie wonder whether she were speaking the whole truth.

'What is your view on this matter, Mrs Carter?' asked Maisie.

'I don't believe for a moment that your Mr Howarth was the prime agent in Bombay, or anything like it,' said Mrs Carter. 'I'd be inclined to look to Mr Leopard, since he had a bit of go about him. However, that's only my opinion, which is based on a five-minute conversation, so I really wouldn't listen to me.' She smiled. 'I believe

Randolph will finish his meeting soon, and tiffin calls. Good day to you both.' She turned, with a swish of her skirts which dislodged another pile of papers, and sailed from the room.

'Now I feel even worse,' said Maisie, staring at the gloves in her hand.

They worked on, sustained by a plate of sandwiches and a jug of lemonade brought by Mr Finnemore. 'Making progress?' he asked, gazing at the four tea chests squatting on the desk, each with a paper label bearing a description scrawled by Maisie.

'I suppose you could say that,' Fraser replied. 'It is slow work, though.'

'Oh it will be,' said Mr Finnemore, with relish. 'It's the sort of painstaking task where you may have to read a document twice, or perhaps even three or four times, before the significance of it dawns on you.'

'And what are you engaged on at present, Mr Finnemore?' asked Maisie.

'Oh, I am compiling a report comparing the administration of the *ryotwari* in Bombay with our use of the *zamindari* in Bengal,' said Mr Finnemore, with shy pride. 'It is a fascinating study; the variations in practice would astonish you.'

'I dare say they would,' said Fraser, 'but we must get on. Thank you, Mr Finnemore.'

Mr Finnemore looked enquiring, but the inspector said no more and he bowed himself out of the room.

'Why did you thank him?' asked Maisie.

For the first time that day, a grin spread across Fraser's

face. 'Why, until Finnemore shared the task which he is engaged in, I had not realised there could be anything worse than what we are doing.'

By five o'clock they had sorted through perhaps two-thirds of the boxes in the room, and assigned the contents. 'So much still to do,' said Maisie, and sighed. 'We haven't even started reading them yet.'

'And don't forget that the Bombay mail will bring more,' said the inspector. 'I hope Hailey exercises some discrimination, and doesn't just stuff in everything he can find.' He looked with loathing at the 'not-relevant' pile teetering on the windowsill. 'Come on, I'll see you to the hotel. I don't know about you, but once I've got the dust of this room out of my bones I don't intend to read or touch a single sheet of paper till we meet again tomorrow.'

'Oh,' said Maisie, 'I thought —'

'Were you expecting us to spend the evening together?' Fraser laughed. 'I thought you'd be sick of me after a whole day in my company, so James and I are playing billiards at the club. I must get out of this building for a couple of hours.'

'I see,' said Maisie. 'In that case you had better go and make yourself ready for Captain James. I'm sure I can find a rickshaw to take me home.'

'Don't be like that, Maisie —'

'*I'm* not being anything,' snapped Maisie. She took off her gloves, which were now grey at the fingertips, put them in the desk drawer, and slammed it shut.

Fraser followed her silently to the entrance, and took her arm as she descended the steps. 'I shall see you home,

Maisie, for the sun is setting.'

'Very well,' muttered Maisie, slightly mollified but determined not to let it show. Once inside the rickshaw he took her hand, and said that it was just the first day, and no doubt things would be much better tomorrow. She let him talk, sensing that his words were perhaps for his own reassurance as much as hers.

The carriage drew up at the stopping-place near her hotel. The inspector got down, and handed her out. 'I shall watch you in,' he said, kissing her hand. 'Goodnight, Maisie, and sleep well.'

'Goodnight, Fraser.' Maisie picked up her skirts and began to walk the short distance to the entrance.

'Psst!' Maisie turned to the place from which the sound had come — a little alley by the side of the hotel — but nothing could be seen except shadows. Then 'Psst!' again, followed by a cough.

Maisie stared. 'I'm not going in there,' she said. 'If you want to speak to me, you come out where I can see you.'

'*Miss Frobisher!*'

Maisie peered into the gloom. 'Who are you? How do you know me?'

'Come in and find out,' whispered the voice — a woman's voice. It made Maisie think of Mrs Carter, though she could not have said why. She took a step forward, and another, and suddenly one of the shadows became a cloaked figure who grabbed her arm.

Maisie squealed, and struggled, and the grip which had seemed so strong suddenly weakened. 'I'm sorry,' the figure muttered. It took a step forward, into the last of the light, and flung back its hood.

Confusion washed over Maisie. 'But I don't —' Bright red hair, and sunburnt skin, just as Ruth had described. Tall and slim, with blue eyes. 'You're the Englishwoman who is looking for me.'

'Yes.' The voice held a note of amusement which made Maisie look again.

'What's going on?' Fraser stood in the mouth of the alley, and the woman stepped quickly into the shadows. 'Who are you, and what do you think you're doing? Tell me this instant, or I'll call the doorman.'

'*No!*' cried Maisie and the woman, together.

'Do you know this woman, Maisie?' asked Fraser, frowning.

'I do now,' said Maisie, still gazing at her. The woman grinned, and Maisie was absolutely sure.

Charlotte Jeroboam.

CHAPTER 5

'It's all right . . . Inspector Hamilton,' said Maisie.

'Then why did you cry out?' Fraser stepped forward and Maisie seized his arm.

'It was nothing, Fraser. I made a mistake.' Miss Jeroboam's cloaked form retreated further into the shadows. 'Please go, or you will miss your appointment.' She slipped her arm through his and led him out of the alley. 'See, I shall go to the hotel now —'

'No you won't,' he said. 'I know that the minute I leave you'll be in the alley talking to whoever that was. What's going on?'

'Nothing is going on,' said Maisie. 'Or at least nothing that you need to know about just yet. Clearly — that person won't talk to me with you here.' She looked up at him. 'Please, go.'

Fraser held her gaze. 'Very well,' he said, and led her

back to the mouth of the alley. 'Wire me later tonight, at Government House, so that I know you're safe. Do you promise?'

'I promise,' said Maisie.

'Good.' Maisie half-expected Fraser to kiss her, as he often did on parting. But he walked to the carriage, and got in. He spoke to the driver, and the carriage moved off.

Maisie peered into the darkness, which was almost velvety in the warm air. 'Are you there?' she asked, timidly.

'Fraser, is it?' said Miss Jeroboam's voice, and Maisie heard advancing footsteps.

'Never mind that,' said Maisie. 'How on earth are you here, and alive?'

'I suppose I ought to be glad that you did not hand me straight over to the inspector,' said Miss Jeroboam. 'I thought that as you gave me a chance before, you might again.'

'I gave you a chance?'

'A chance to die.' Another step, and another, and Miss Jeroboam advanced into the dim light. 'But now I am asking you for something different.'

Maisie blinked. 'What do you want?'

'A chance to live.'

***

Maisie was shocked when she saw Charlotte Jeroboam in the harsh electric light of her room. Her clothes beneath her cloak were as odd as Ruth had said; but that was not what distressed Maisie. 'Would you like a hot bath?' she asked.

'Am I so filthy?' Miss Jeroboam laughed, then gasped

for breath. 'I can see from the horror you're so careful to disguise that I am.' She strolled to Maisie's bedroom door, opened it, and peered in. 'Very nice. Is the bathroom beyond?' Without waiting for an answer she walked in and threw the door open. The next sound was a gush of water.

'Are you hungry?'

'Starving.' The bathroom door closed, and Miss Jeroboam began to cough again.

Maisie shrugged to herself, and rang the bell. When the pageboy arrived she ordered a generous dinner and half a bottle of wine. His eyebrows lifted, but he did not comment, for which Maisie was glad. 'Oh, and could you send a wire for me?' She caught up a pencil and scribbled on a sheet of hotel notepaper: *Mr Hamilton, Government House. Safe at hotel — M.*

'Is that all, ma'am?'

'Yes, for now,' said Maisie, and closed the door. She sat down at the dressing table and unpinned her hat, then rose, locked the door on the inside, and sat in the armchair.

She heard gentle splashing, and resigned herself to a long wait; but within ten minutes Miss Jeroboam peeked round the door, her red hair soaking wet and flattened to her head. 'Do you mind if I use one of your towels?' she asked. 'Some red may come off —'

'Oh, for heaven's sake,' said Maisie. 'You've come back from the dead. A towel is neither here nor there.'

'I hoped you would say that,' replied Miss Jeroboam, 'for otherwise I should probably make a frightful mess of your robe.' She smiled and disappeared, to return wearing Maisie's silk kimono, her hair wrapped in a towel.

'Sit,' said Maisie, indicating the other chair, 'and tell me.'

'Tell you what?' Miss Jeroboam sat down, then swung her legs up and crossed them. With her towel and robe she looked rather like a strange new goddess. Her breath rattled, but she did not cough.

'Everything.'

'When I jumped off the rail of that ship I honestly meant to die,' said Miss Jeroboam, her blue eyes gazing beyond Maisie to a distant horizon. 'I desired nothing more than oblivion. I remember hitting the water and unlacing my boots, and even as I did, asking myself what I was doing. But I kicked them off, and got out of my petticoats, and then my head broke the surface. The ship was already some way in the distance. If I had called, you would not have heard. So it was just me, and the water, and the darkness. I trod water, and my body conspired to keep me afloat for quite a while; but eventually my legs were too tired to kick. I remember swallowing that first mouthful of seawater, but nothing more.' She paused. 'Do you want me to go on?'

Maisie swallowed, and nodded.

'When I came to I thought that I had died and gone to hell, for I could feel my skin boiling on my bones. Then I heard voices, speaking a language of which I recognised a word or two, and opened my eyes. I was in a boat — a fishing boat, from the look of it. Someone saw me stirring, and at once they all began rejoicing and offering me water and food. One man waved a piece of wood in my face, and eventually I made out that I had been holding onto that when they rescued me. A few days later, I am not sure how many, we landed in their own village which they told me was a day's walk from Bombay. They were very hospitable; but I am afraid that I stayed only until I was strong enough to make the journey to Bombay. I ate a last meal, borrowed some money, and set out for the city.'

'And what about…?' Maisie touched her own hair.

'Oh, that.' Miss Jeroboam unwrapped the towel and fingered a strand of bright copper hair. 'I took a train partway to Bombay, and the first thing I saw at the station bookstall was a newspaper headline that I was dead.' She laughed. 'At that point I had not decided my course of action; so I bought henna at the market and for a few annas more, the stall owner helped me dye my hair. I had seen myself in a foxed old mirror at one of the fishermen's houses, and I hoped that different hair, along with my changed appearance, would be sufficient to prevent anyone recognising me.' She touched her cheek, and winced. 'I survived from day to day, begging scraps of food in the late evening, and, I am afraid, stealing what I could. But as I began to grow stronger, I realised that this was no life at all, and that my hopes rested on finding one person.' Her eyes met Maisie's. 'You.'

'I see,' said Maisie, feeling dazed.

'Yes,' said Miss Jeroboam. 'Because —'

She jumped up at a knock on the door, and with a look of utter panic on her face, ran into Maisie's bedroom and pulled the door closed.

'Yes, who is it?' called Maisie.

'It is I, with your dinner, madam.' Maisie recognised

the page's voice.

'Oh, of course!' Maisie rose and unbolted the door. 'Just leave the tray on the table, please.'

The page did as he was told, but Maisie noticed him eyeing the bedroom door. 'That will be all, thank you,' she said pointedly. 'I shall leave the tray outside when I have finished.'

Miss Jeroboam waited until Maisie had re-locked the door before emerging from the bedroom, rather shamefaced.

'You must be hungry,' said Maisie. She looked at the tray, on which was one plate and, with the half bottle of wine, one glass. She shrugged, and went to the bedroom for her water glass.

'I can wait,' said Miss Jeroboam; but her eyes were on the plate of food.

'Don't be silly,' said Maisie. 'Sit down.' She moved the armchair bedside the table and motioned to her guest. Miss Jeroboam hesitated, then obeyed, and within five minutes the plate was cleared.

'So,' said Maisie, pouring them both a glass of wine, 'you said that your hopes rested on me.'

'They do,' said Miss Jeroboam, taking a sip of wine. That made her cough, and it took her a little while to recover. 'I knew that if anyone recognised me, it would take no time for word to spread that the famous lady explorer was not dead — and once that discovery was made, then soon I would be either dead, or in prison. You had helped me, in your own way, and I thought that you might again.' She sipped her wine and regarded Maisie.

'Do you remember a conversation we had on the promenade deck of the *Britannia*? You asked me if I could find a female patron, and I laughed at the idea.'

Maisie nodded. 'I do.'

'I wondered if you might — not be my patron, as such, but intercede for me with the powers that be. I enquired for you but I had to be discreet, and by the time I found your hotel you had departed for Calcutta. *Very well*, I thought, *then so shall I*. I secured the money for a servant's ticket on the mail train — please don't ask how — and here I am.'

'But what do you want from me?' asked Maisie. 'To whom do you wish me to speak?'

Miss Jeroboam's blue eyes rested on hers. 'Given that you were with Inspector Hamilton, and he mentioned Government House, I assume that the pair of you have business there at a high level. This is what I want. In exchange for anything that I can tell of how I was recruited, and what I did, I ask for — not quite a pardon.' She sighed, and even that small movement brought on another cough. 'As you have probably noticed, my seafaring adventure has not agreed with me. I do not know how long I have left, and I do not want to spend that time looking over my shoulder. The best I can hope for —' she said it very steadily — 'is a letter from the viceroy guaranteeing me safe passage. I desire nothing more than to undertake the expedition I had planned, in the swamp-forests of Bombay, and to end my days in search of the flora and fauna I had dedicated my life to before I was tempted.'

'I see,' said Maisie.

'Is that a no?' said Miss Jeroboam, setting down her wineglass. 'Then let me get changed, and I shall go, and you will not see me again —'

'No!' cried Maisie. 'Please, stay. It isn't a no, not at all. It's just —'

'You weren't expecting me?' Miss Jeroboam smiled.

'Well, no,' said Maisie, smiling back. 'I truly thought you were dead.' She crossed the room, knelt beside Miss Jeroboam's chair, and took her hand. It was raw, and blistered, and the nails were broken. She looked up at Miss Jeroboam's face, embarrassed for her, and saw purple shadows under her eyes. 'You must be exhausted,' she said. 'Stay here, and we shall go and see the viceroy in the morning.'

'Really?' Miss Jeroboam blinked at her. Then she yawned, covering her mouth with her other hand. 'I am so tired,' she murmured.

Maisie smiled. 'I'm not surprised,' she said. 'And yes, really.'

Half an hour later she looked down at Charlotte Jeroboam, sound asleep on the chaise longue. Her breathing was regular, but ragged, with a catch in it, and every so often she would start, murmur something, and settle again. Maisie sighed to herself, went into the bedroom, and made herself ready for the night, for of course she would not be ringing for Ruth. *What will the viceroy say,* she asked herself as she lay in bed, trying to ignore the rumbling of her stomach. *And what on earth will Fraser say?* Her heart beat quickly, and Maisie told herself that it was excitement, and wholly natural; but she shivered a little, even in the warm Calcutta night, and she could not have said why.

CHAPTER 6

'Should we have warned him?' asked Miss Jeroboam, as the closed carriage rattled through the streets. The sky was light, but the city so quiet that the carriage seemed to make a fearful noise. *Enough to wake the dead*, thought Maisie.

'How could I warn him?' asked Maisie. 'All I could do would be to send him a telegram, and anything I put in that would either alert his staff or make no sense at all.'

Miss Jeroboam pulled her cloak more closely around her, and Maisie continued to look out at the pale, silent city.

Maisie had passed an uneasy night. Every so often she started awake, convinced someone was in the room; she heard rustling, and her blood froze; then she realised it was only Miss Jeroboam, sleeping in the adjoining room. *I must tell the viceroy as soon as I can*, she thought each time, turning her pillow and rearranging her covers. *If I have to keep this secret for long, I shall explode.*

Already she felt guilty that she had not confided in Fraser; but what was she to do? Miss Jeroboam would not speak with him present. She would speak to no one, except Maisie and the viceroy.

Maisie had almost screamed at a light touch on her shoulder. 'We should go early,' Miss Jeroboam had said, 'before people are generally about.' Maisie had peered at her face, shielded by the hood of her cloak, and wondered what sort of half-life Miss Jeroboam had led while trying to find her.

The page Maisie knew had not been on duty when she rang that morning, and one of the night staff was sitting at the desk.

'Miss Frobisher?' he asked, his finger poised on his task list.

'That's right,' said Maisie. 'Is the carriage ready?'

'Indeed it is, madam,' he replied. 'May I ask where you are going?'

'I have a business appointment,' said Maisie. She heard Miss Jeroboam's footsteps crossing the foyer behind her, and asked the attendant for a copy of the evening menu to distract him. Then she made her way to the carriage, its horses snorting and stamping themselves awake.

The flight of stairs leading to the door of Government House seemed to take an eternity to climb. Maisie questioned her decision on every step, and those steps were not quick, for Miss Jeroboam did not spring up the stairs as once she would have done. She went slowly. Maisie could hear her breathing, and an occasional cough shook her slim frame till Maisie feared she would topple.

'Would you like my arm?' she asked, with a pang of guilt that now she was the strong person assisting the weaker.

'I can manage perfectly well,' said Charlotte Jeroboam; but she stopped while she said it, and then continued to climb, her mouth in a firm, straight line.

At the door, a footman regarded them with disdain. 'No general business is permitted here until ten o'clock at the earliest,' he said, looking down his nose at Maisie and her companion.

'We are not general business,' replied Maisie. She fumbled in her bag, and brought out her card case and a pencil. On the back of the card she scribbled: *Imperative that I see you at once — MF*. 'Could you give this to the viceroy, please?' she said, passing it over. 'I guarantee that if he discovers that you failed to admit us, he will be most displeased.' The footman raised his eyebrows at her, leaned back to take in the cloaked figure of Miss Jeroboam, and departed, none too quickly.

A few minutes later he returned. 'Please come this way, madam.'

Maisie found herself once more in the waiting room she knew. Miss Jeroboam wandered about, looking at the photographs, the furnishings, and the view. Maisie suspected she was too nervous to see it.

Miss Jeroboam swung round. 'What is he like, the viceroy?'

Maisie considered. 'Fair, I think. Principled. Torn, perhaps.'

'That's an interesting word,' Miss Jeroboam commented. 'Would you say he is merciful?'

Maisie remembered the bargain Lord Strathcairn had struck with Mr Howarth. 'In the right circumstances, yes.'

She looked up to find Miss Jeroboam regarding her with amusement. 'How far you have come, Maisie,' she said. 'I thought you were such a silly thing when you bustled into the dining room in your yellow silk, and look at you now.' Maisie couldn't quite read her expression. She saw pride, but there was a glint of something else. Something not as nice. Was it — jealousy?

The door opened abruptly. 'Do you know what time it is, Miss Frobisher?' demanded the viceroy. He motioned to them to sit, and without waiting, seated himself on the nearest chair. 'I have not even breakfasted.' He started as his eyes fell on Miss Jeroboam. 'Who is this?'

'I apologise, Your Excellency,' said Maisie. 'Allow me to introduce my former shipmate, Miss Charlotte Jeroboam.'

***

'You're sure?' asked Fraser. 'You're absolutely sure?'

'Yes,' said Maisie, 'I am. At first I hardly knew her, with the red hair, and her sunburn, but once you look past that, her eyes and her features are exactly the same.'

'Including the ears?'

'I must admit,' said Maisie gravely, 'that I have not studied Miss Jeroboam's ears as yet. But it is her. She knew I wore yellow silk on my first night at the captain's table.'

Fraser began to rise, then sat down again. 'Someone

could have told her that,' he said, pushing his hair from his brow.

'Who, exactly? You have seen how she is dressed. She hasn't been chatting to the Smythes or the Fortescues.'

'I know.' Fraser sighed. 'It's just — beyond comprehension. Beyond sense.' Suddenly he laughed, a short sharp laugh which was almost a bark. 'That would explain why she stepped into the shadows when she saw me. I suppose I am hardly her favourite person.' He raised his eyebrows. 'Come to that, I am not sure you are. After all, Maisie, you were the one who sealed her fate.'

'It isn't up to me to establish her motives,' Maisie replied. 'And before that happened, she was my friend. Sometimes my only friend on the ship.'

Fraser regarded her for some time. 'At least that has turned out well.' He consulted his watch. 'When did you say you got here?'

'At about seven o'clock,' said Maisie.

'And now it is practically ten,' said Fraser. He surveyed the boxes of papers which, so far that morning, neither had touched.

'You don't know how much she has to tell,' said Maisie. She walked to the window and gazed at Calcutta, bathed in morning sunshine and looking its usual self, compared with the landscape which had seemed so alien earlier.

A tap at the door made them both draw themselves up, but they relaxed when a picture hat appeared, followed by the head of Mrs Carter. 'Only me,' she said, coming into the room and shutting the door behind her. 'That was a surprise.' She eyed the inspector, who sprang up and placed a chair for her.

'Have you seen Miss Jeroboam, Mrs Carter?' asked Maisie.

'Yes,' said Mrs Carter, meditatively. 'She isn't what I expected.' She sat down, and placed her large handbag on her lap. 'Miss Frobisher, won't you ask me what I expected?'

Maisie laughed. 'Please take it as read.'

'Well,' said Mrs Carter, 'I thought she would be a dashing young thing, rather a smart and forceful young lady. Not that I believe the accounts in the newspapers, you understand, but one must base one's expectations on something.' She looked at Maisie as if sizing her up. 'Lord Strathcairn and I have been talking to her for the last hour.'

'And?' asked Fraser.

'And she has done her best to furnish us with information,' said Mrs Carter. 'But there is a parallel with your erstwhile colleague Mr Howarth, and also a difference.'

The pair waited until they could bear it no longer. 'Well?' asked Fraser.

'Your friend Mr Howarth thought he was giving us absolutely everything we could wish for; but as it turned out, he had less than half the story, and never knew it.' Mrs Carter's eyes glinted. 'Miss Jeroboam, also, it seems, wishes to give us the whole story, but she cannot. Often, when she comes to a piece of information, she frowns, and thinks, and tells us that it is gone. The viceroy and I have asked in as many ways as we know how, and approached the subject from all the angles we can think of, but part of

Miss Jeroboam's memory remains obstinately blank.'

The inspector's eyes narrowed. 'Do you believe her, Mrs Carter?'

Mrs Carter considered. 'I am not sure. She is convincing, very convincing, but —' She gazed at Maisie. 'I do not know her as you do, Miss Frobisher.'

The inspector turned to Maisie. 'You have spent more time with her than anyone else, Maisie,' he said. 'Last night, and this morning, was there anything to suggest that Miss Jeroboam's intentions might not be honourable?'

Maisie looked at her hands, clasped tightly in her lap. 'She has been through so much,' she said softly. 'I'm sure you have seen for yourself, Mrs Carter, that she is unwell.'

'Well yes, if I had almost drowned I dare say I should be unwell too,' said Mrs Carter. 'Did you see anything to make you think she may know more than she admits, or have any motive other than a simple exchange of information for a pardon?'

Maisie stared at her hands until she barely recognised them, but it didn't help at all. Memories of last night flashed through her mind; Miss Jeroboam's cheerfulness, her ridiculous concern for Maisie's towel, and the clear-eyed calculation with which she had worked out her bargain.

She looked up, and met Mrs Carter's eyes. 'I don't know.'

CHAPTER 7

'I thought as much,' said Mrs Carter, rising. 'We mustn't keep the viceroy waiting.'

Maisie stared. 'We're meeting with the viceroy?'

'*You* are,' Mrs Carter replied. 'Didn't I say?'

Fraser rose, too. 'As I was part of the team who attempted to bring Miss Jeroboam to justice in the first place, Mrs Carter, I ought to be party to this conversation.' He glanced at Maisie.

'I think Inspector Hamilton should, too,' said Maisie, feeling it was expected of her.

Mrs Carter considered him. 'The viceroy said Miss Frobisher, quite distinctly,' she said. 'However, it will do no harm to bring you too.' As she swept from the room Fraser raised his eyebrows at Maisie, who shrugged, not knowing what to say.

Mrs Carter led them through the tangle of corridors and

staircases to a room Maisie had seen once or twice before; the viceroy's study. She knocked, and entered. 'Here is Miss Frobisher, and Inspector Hamilton too,' she said, her voice level.

'Hamilton too, hey?' Lord Strathcairn scrutinised them. 'Perhaps that is for the best.' Maisie sneaked a glance at Fraser as they entered the room, and detected a distinct smirk hovering about his mouth. 'Sit yourselves down, do.'

'Where is Miss Jeroboam, Your Excellency?' asked Maisie.

'She is resting,' said the viceroy. 'Mrs Carter and I have fairly worn her out with questions. My doctor ought to take a look at her; but she will not hear of it.' He paused. 'Perhaps in a few days, when she is stronger.' His eyes met Maisie's. 'I have decided the best course of action is to allocate Miss Jeroboam a set of rooms in Government House, at least for the time being. Changed though she is, if she were allowed free movement in Calcutta, having someone recognise her by chance would reduce her effectiveness considerably.'

'You are sure it is her, Your Excellency?' asked Fraser.

'Oh yes,' said the viceroy, quickly. 'Her story checks out, and she remembers enough to be reasonably convincing. Possibly she will recall more, in time.' He sighed. 'We shall have to be patient with her; and patience is not a virtue I have in abundance.' Then he smiled. 'Even in her current semi-invalid state, though, Miss Jeroboam can be of use to us. She gave me a description of the man who recruited her in London, and he sounds uncommonly like our man Leopard, or De Souza.'

'Oh!' breathed Maisie.

'Oh, indeed,' said the viceroy drily. 'You might say that Miss Jeroboam has turned up at exactly the right time; for the Bombay mail will get in on Monday, and travelling on it is a visiting dignitary for whom I am obliged to hold a reception.' He rolled his eyes. 'At least it is not another dinner. I had already invited Leopard to the reception, and my plan was to ask you, Miss Frobisher, to engage him in conversation.' He paused. 'I believe I am right in thinking that, when Howarth was apprehended near the cathedral, Leopard did not see you?'

'That is correct,' said Maisie. Suddenly the room seemed too warm, and she gripped the arms of her chair to steady herself. 'Does Miss Jeroboam's arrival mean that you no longer require me to do so?'

'Far from it,' said Lord Strathcairn. 'I intend to invite Miss Jeroboam to the reception, put her in a quiet corner, perhaps with Hamilton here to attend to her, and have you bring Leopard within her sights. A positive identification would be a great help to us.' He sighed. 'After you identified him from the photograph I placed a watch on him, and his local post office have reported the contents of all his mail, both incoming and outgoing.' The viceroy snorted. 'I might as well not have bothered, for according to their reports he is as innocent as a babe in arms.'

'So there have been no attempts to communicate with Howarth?' asked the inspector. 'I believe Leopard said when they met that he would contact Howarth once he had checked the document, and arrange a reward.'

'Not a thing.' Lord Strathcairn leaned back in his chair.

'I thought the trail had gone cold, so Miss Jeroboam could not possibly have arrived at a better time. That, in itself, worries me.' He gazed out of the window. 'So get your collars starched and your petticoats ironed, or whatever it is that you young people do, ready for Monday. I shall issue you with a formal invitation, of course, via Captain James.' He smiled. 'In the meantime, though, you both have a job to do. Miss Frobisher, I want you to find out as much as you can about Anton De Souza. His hobbies, his interests, what he likes to eat and drink, the books and plays he enjoys. You must be as congenial a companion as you possibly can.'

'I see,' said Maisie, rather taken aback.

'I thought you would,' said the viceroy. 'I daresay you have plenty of information in those boxes of yours, but I shall get an additional dossier prepared for you, to save time.'

'And what am I to do, Your Excellency?' asked Fraser.

'Oh, your job is far harder, Inspector Hamilton,' said the viceroy. 'I need you to convince Miss Jeroboam that you mean her no harm, and that you have her best interests at heart.' His mouth puckered in a schoolboyish way. 'I am not sure why, considering that you both had a substantial hand in her downfall, but Miss Jeroboam sees *you*, Hamilton, as the villain of the piece. However, if you are to look after her with any success, she has to trust you.' He nodded. 'I suggest that the pair of you see her this afternoon, talk to her gently, and then Miss Frobisher can leave you to begin the process.'

Fraser said nothing.

Lord Strathcairn regarded him from under his eyebrows. 'All clear, Inspector Hamilton?'

'Oh yes, Your Excellency,' said Fraser, his face expressionless. 'All clear.'

'Good.' The viceroy opened his desk drawer and took out a bundle of papers. 'Now if you'll excuse me, this business, promising as it is, has already postponed one meeting, and I have no doubt that Captain James is holding back a flood of petitioners somewhere in the building.' He reached into his jacket pocket, put on a pair of spectacles, and thus signalled that the meeting was at an end.

'Will you be at the reception, Mrs Carter?' asked Maisie, as they walked along the corridor.

'Certainly not,' said Mrs Carter. 'Since Randolph and I accosted your Mr Howarth with Leopard, on the last occasion he was seen in public, I hardly think it would be wise for us to pop up at a reception where you will be using your feminine wiles to put him at ease.'

'Please don't say that,' said Maisie. 'I shall be civil, and interested, and hopefully interesting, but nothing more.'

'I should think not,' said Fraser. He grinned. 'Apart from anything else, Miss Frobisher, you are already married.'

Mrs Carter opened her eyes very wide. 'I beg your pardon?'

'It is just a joke between us, Mrs Carter,' said Maisie hurriedly.

'I see,' said Mrs Carter, her nose wrinkling as if she detected an unfamiliar smell. 'Don't let your attempts at humour get in the way of your work. Either of you.' She consulted the watch strapped on her surprisingly slim wrist. 'Randolph and I are attending a lunchtime concert, so I shall leave you here.' She pursed her lips. 'I shall see if Ainsley is free on Monday night, and if so, get him an invitation. He is a useful man to have about. Good eyes, and ears.'

'Thank you, Mrs Carter.' Maisie smiled at her, grateful that as well as the inspector, she would have another friendly face at the reception.

'Don't mention it.' Mrs Carter opened her handbag, pulled out a concert programme and a pair of pince nez, and sailed off, gazing at the one through the other.

'How are you feeling?' asked Maisie, as they walked slowly down the corridor together.

Fraser did not answer her at once, but strolled along, hands in pockets. 'A mixture of relieved and frustrated, I suppose.'

Now it was Maisie's turn to pause while she considered what to say in reply. 'Why?' she said, eventually.

'If nothing else, at least we can escape from that paper-stuffed room for a while.'

'And the frustration?' Maisie ventured.

Fraser stopped dead in the middle of the corridor and stared at her. 'What do you think, Maisie? You'll be getting to grips with Leopard, while I have been ordered to ingratiate myself with Charlotte Jeroboam for the purpose of playing chaperone.' His brow furrowed, and his grey eyes flashed silver in the glare of the electric light. 'If you didn't come to India to work in an office, I definitely didn't come to India for *this*.' He strode off without a backward glance, leaving Maisie standing in the middle of the corridor, utterly perplexed.

CHAPTER 8

'Please keep still, Miss Maisie,' said Ruth, around a hairpin. 'Otherwise you'll be lopsided, and I won't answer for the consequences.'

'Sorry, Ruth,' said Maisie, turning and eliciting a tut of disapproval from her maid. 'I'm feeling nervous.'

Ruth pushed in another hairpin. 'There's no call to be nervous. How many receptions and parties and dinners have you attended since you arrived in India?' She fell silent, and when Maisie looked in the mirror, Ruth was regarding her critically. 'Is it to do with Inspector Hamilton?'

'I suppose you could say that,' said Maisie.

Ruth smirked visibly. 'Oh well, in that case it isn't my place to comment,' she said, sliding the last hairpin into place. 'There. Pretty as a picture, though I wish you hadn't spent the last few days shut up in your room with books.

You've lost some of your bloom.'

'It wasn't my choice, believe me,' said Maisie. 'Just — something I needed to do.'

The dossier the viceroy procured had stated that Leopard's favourite author was Sir Walter Scott, and as Maisie had read but a few of Scott's novels, and that some time ago, she had borrowed a set from Government House and set to work. Her evenings had been taken up with concerts and plays of the kind he preferred, and all in all she felt rather drowned in culture.

A further side-effect was that she had seen little of Inspector Hamilton. His time had been divided between visits to Miss Jeroboam and fact-finding in their office. Maisie had invited him to a concert, but he had declined. 'Having eaten, slept and breathed Anton De Souza for the past few days, I have no intention of spending my evenings with him too,' he had said, as he put his notes in the drawer and closed it.

'But you'd be spending the evening with me,' said Maisie.

Fraser looked at her, then away. 'At the moment, that is almost the same thing. Now if you'll excuse me, I'll lock this room and be on my way.'

Their first joint meeting with Miss Jeroboam had not gone particularly well. Maisie had been admitted to Miss Jeroboam's sitting room with a smile, but when she mentioned another visitor, Miss Jeroboam's face closed instantly. 'I am too weak for more than one visitor at a time,' she said, putting the book she was reading face-down in her lap. 'Tell them to go away, Maisie.'

'Won't you try, Charlotte, just for a few minutes?'

Miss Jeroboam looked suspicious. 'Who is it?'

Maisie bit her lip. 'Inspector Hamilton.' Miss Jeroboam scowled. 'Before you say no, he hasn't come to shout at you, or accuse you of anything. He is here to help, just as I am.'

Miss Jeroboam considered. 'I want five minutes alone with you first, Maisie, and then I shall decide.'

'Very well,' said Maisie. 'I shall go and let him know.'

'Don't bring him back in with you.' The words rang out in the quiet room.

Outside, Fraser glowered. 'I shall say nothing,' he muttered. 'I don't trust myself to speak, frankly.'

'We must give her time,' said Maisie. 'Five minutes is nothing.'

'To you, perhaps,' said Fraser. 'Very well, you go and be a ministering angel.' The last remark was slightly louder, and Maisie suspected Miss Jeroboam was intended to hear it.

She gave no sign of it, though, when Maisie re-entered the room. 'Would you like something to drink? Lemonade, or tea…'

'Only if you do,' said Maisie. She was relieved that the conversation was proceeding along normal lines; but the ludicrousness of the situation — paying a call on a returned fugitive from justice — struck her all of a sudden, and she couldn't help smiling.

'That's better,' said Miss Jeroboam. 'Now, tell me about Bombay.'

Maisie did her best, concentrating on the pleasure trips

she had taken, the elephant rides, the events at Government House. She wanted to tell Miss Jeroboam everything; but it did not feel safe. And in her mind's eye was Fraser, fuming and fidgeting outside the door.

'You are capital entertainment for an invalid, Miss Frobisher,' Miss Jeroboam remarked. 'Your entertaining conversation diverts me, but there is nothing to alarm or distress. If you ever lose your fortune, you could certainly find work as a companion.'

'You're too kind,' Maisie replied. She consulted her watch. 'My five minutes are up.'

'Are they?' Miss Jeroboam glanced at the clock on the mantelpiece. 'I miss my wristwatch,' she said. 'Then again, it is only one of many things I have lost.' She studied Maisie. 'I never thought I should be anything but young and strong, and look at me.' Her mouth twisted in disgust.

'I am sure that if you rest, and follow the doctor's instructions, you will recover your health by and by,' said Maisie. 'Have you seen a doctor?'

Miss Jeroboam shrugged. 'I don't see the point. The doctor will tell me what I already know; that I'm fit for nothing. Useless.'

'You're not useless!' exclaimed Maisie. 'The information you have already given will be very useful. And Inspector Hamilton and I can explain how you could help further.'

'I can't see him,' said Miss Jeroboam. 'I don't feel well enough. You have tired me out.' She leaned back in her chair and closed her eyes.

Maisie heard a creak on the other side of the door.

'Charlotte,' she said. Miss Jeroboam opened her eyes. 'You must try. I give you my word that he is here to help, and if you let him explain, you will see that too.'

'Your word, hmm?' Miss Jeroboam's eyes narrowed. 'I suppose that is worth something.'

Her words stung Maisie like a slap. 'Let me be frank, Miss Jeroboam. You are seeking free passage and the right to live as you choose. The viceroy is under no obligation to grant that. Therefore if you wish to leave Government House, you may have to do things you would rather not. Now, will you see Inspector Hamilton . . . or not?'

Miss Jeroboam's fair eyebrows, such an odd contrast with her bright-red hair, drew together. 'Since I have no choice, I had better get it over with, hadn't I?' She looked at the door. 'You can stop skulking outside, Inspector, and come in.'

After a slight pause, Inspector Hamilton did as he was told. Maisie glanced at his face, and her heart sank. If he had looked merely annoyed she could have smoothed things over; but his face showed the same blankness as it had in the viceroy's study. Only the slight flush high on his cheeks betrayed his fury.

'Well, isn't this nice,' said Miss Jeroboam. 'Won't you sit down, Inspector? Caught any good criminals lately?'

The inspector took his seat before replying. 'One or two, thank you, Miss Jeroboam. How is your specimen-hunting going?'

'Oh, it is fascinating,' said Miss Jeroboam. 'I have been observing a most interesting example of a familiar species which I have not seen for some time.' She paused. 'A captive male of the species displaying unusually submissive behaviour. Studying the conditions promoting this unusual phenomenon would be time well spent.'

'Actually I would like some lemonade,' said Maisie. She rose, not daring to look at Fraser, and rang the bell.

The remainder of the visit had lasted as long as it took Maisie to drink a glass of lemonade. Fraser had said nothing more, and had spent the remainder of his time staring out of the window. As soon as they were out of earshot, he had muttered, 'See? Pointless,' and strode back to what was now his office.

Maisie had visited Miss Jeroboam briefly on two more occasions. Once she had mentioned the reception, and said that she was looking forward to it, but apart from that they had spoken of general matters. Maisie had tried once or twice to allude to the past; but whenever she did Miss Jeroboam grimaced as if Maisie had touched on a sore spot, and Maisie hastily steered the conversation towards trivialities.

But now it was the evening of the reception; the time when all her study, all her preparation, must bear fruit. Maisie spent most of the journey reciting the names of Scott's novels, along with their main characters. If nothing else, it kept her mind off the reality that soon she would be meeting Leopard, and hearing that hypnotic voice directed at her.

Captain James welcomed her at the door. 'Good evening, Miss Frobisher,' he said. 'Let me take your shawl. Is that a new dress in our honour? Indeed, you are looking even more dazzling than usual.'

'You flatterer.' Maisie laughed. 'I see you have polished your epaulettes for the occasion.'

'Indeed I have,' said the captain, smiling. 'They are so brilliant that I declare you can see your face in them.' He leaned down so that Maisie could try, and as she stood on tiptoe he murmured 'Good luck' in her ear. 'Sadly it is not a dancing occasion, or I would claim you as a partner later.'

'Such a disappointment,' said Maisie, and walked into the hallway, chin held high.

The footman directed her into a different room from usual, set out in an unexpected way. It was still large, but less brilliantly lit, and the space was divided by screens, so that it appeared as a series of interconnecting rooms. Within each space was placed an assortment of chairs and settees, grouped to encourage conversation.

The waiter supplied Maisie with a glass of champagne, and she drifted from space to space, searching for a face she knew. She came across Miss Jeroboam in a dark corner. Her bright hair was elaborately arranged, so that a casual observer would see the hair rather than the face beneath it, and she wore a fussy dress which Maisie felt sure she would never have chosen for herself. Maisie started as she saw Fraser, sitting nearby, for he sported a large moustache not dissimilar to the viceroy's, and his hair was parted differently. *Of course; he is hiding from Leopard.* Fraser caught her eye, then looked away. *I am not supposed to know him*, thought Maisie, and wandered off.

Where is Leopard? She remembered him wearing a linen suit; but the dossier had said that he tended to wear a loose silk suit on formal occasions. She scanned the room for a tall, portly, dark-haired man. There were many; and Maisie resigned herself to roaming until she found the right one. She had traversed almost the whole room when her eye fell on Mr Ainsley, very correctly dressed in white tie and tails, chatting to a man of the right description with his back to her. Maisie swallowed, and advanced.

'Mr Ainsley, how lovely to see you again!' she exclaimed. 'How are you enjoying Calcutta?'

The man turned, and Maisie braced herself. After the initial shock of recognition, he seemed younger than she remembered.

Mr Ainsley stepped forward and kissed Maisie's hand. 'Calcutta is most impressive, but of course immeasurably enhanced by your presence, my dear. De Souza, allow me to introduce Miss Maisie Frobisher, who has arrived in India quite recently. Miss Frobisher, may I present Mr De Souza.'

'Delighted to meet you,' said Maisie, curtsying and offering her hand. Mr De Souza took it, and raised it to his lips, and then the words *Miss Frobisher*, pronounced very distinctly behind him, made him pause.

A nervous-looking footman cleared his throat. 'I do apologise for interrupting, Miss Frobisher, but Captain James asked me to find you.' He made an unmistakable motion with his head.

'Do excuse me,' said Maisie, with as charming a smile as she could manage, and followed the footman to a discreet distance. 'What is it?'

'There's a gentleman at the door,' quavered the

footman. 'He doesn't have an invitation, but he says that you know him. Captain James apologises, but he does have a letter, and we would rather not turn him away if he ought to be here —'

Maisie glanced back at the two gentlemen, who were trying not to appear interested, then at the agonised footman. She sighed. 'Very well,' she said, and followed him, too annoyed by the interruption to dwell on the cause of it.

'He is in there with Captain James,' said the footman, pointing to the now-familiar waiting room. Maisie picked up her skirts and crossed to the door, through which she could hear voices — not raised, not angry, not stern. She tapped, and entered.

'Ah, there you are, Miss Frobisher,' said Captain James. 'This gentleman says you will vouch for him. Is he correct?' He turned to his left, where a fair-haired young man in a dress suit was sitting, pulling at his moustache and looking even more awkward than usual.

Edward Mandeville.

CHAPTER 9

'Maisie!' Edward Mandeville jumped to his feet. 'How lovely to see you! I hoped you'd be here.'

'Mr Mandeville,' said Maisie. 'What a . . . surprise.'

'Oh dear,' said Mr Mandeville. 'You're cross with me, aren't you? I do apologise.'

'So I take it Mr Mandeville is who he says he is,' said Captain James, looking from one to the other.

'Who does he say he is?' asked Maisie.

Mr Mandeville drew himself up to his full height. 'An employee of the Indian Civil Service, working for Lord Montgomery in Bombay. Here.' He passed Maisie a letter, and as she unfolded the heavy paper Maisie recognised Lord Montgomery's seal.

Strathcairn, I'm sending Mandeville over — he will tell you the reason why himself. Some information would be

very welcome, if you would be so kind.
Yours, Montgomery

'This appears correct,' said Maisie. 'I can vouch that Mr Mandeville is an employee of the Civil Service in Bombay.'

'Excellent,' said Captain James, rising. 'In that case, Mandeville, why don't you thank Miss Frobisher by taking her into the reception?'

'Shall we?' asked Edward Mandeville, crooking an arm, and Maisie, fuming, had no choice but to take it.

'This is just like one of the governor's dos in Bombay!' he exclaimed as they entered the reception. 'I thought it would be bigger, somehow.'

'I suppose a governor is a governor, wherever he is,' said Maisie absently, her eyes searching the room for Mr De Souza. 'If you don't mind, I was in the middle of an interesting conversation.'

'Oh, were you? Terribly sorry.' Edward Mandeville gazed around the room too, though Maisie could not work out who he was looking for. 'Is Howarth here?'

Maisie started, and hoped he hadn't noticed. 'Mr Howarth? I haven't seen him.' She paused. 'This reception is a little smaller than the usual ones. Or he may be out surveying. Thinking about it, I haven't seen him for a while.'

'That'll be me, when I return,' said Edward Mandeville, puffing out his chest. 'How's Hamilton getting on? I suppose he is surveying too, if Howarth is looking after him.'

'I couldn't say,' said Maisie vaguely. 'Edward, could you be an angel and find me a glass of champagne from somewhere? I put mine down when I was summoned to vouch for you, and I daresay it has been consumed by now.'

'But of course!' Edward exclaimed. He scanned the room, shading his eyes as he did so, and departed from her side with a bound.

'Thank heavens for that,' muttered Maisie, and set off in pursuit of Leopard.

She found Mr De Souza still chatting companionably with Mr Ainsley. 'I'm so sorry about that,' she said as she approached. 'I was called away.'

'Indeed you were,' said Mr De Souza. 'Now, where were we?' Maisie bobbed and gave him her hand, and he kissed it gently.

'Mr De Souza and I were discussing trade in Calcutta,' said Mr Ainsley. 'We have contacts in common in the merchant line.'

'Oh, how nice,' said Maisie. 'What is your line, Mr De Souza?'

'Oh, I dabble,' he replied. 'A bit of this, a bit of that. I am never *all in*, as they say.'

'A wise strategy, both in card games and in trade,' said Mr Ainsley. 'I have suffered many a time through lack of diversity. In a country such as this one can never trust the rivers not to burst their banks, or the crops not to fail.'

'It must be a hazardous way of living,' said Maisie.

Mr De Souza twinkled at her. 'No more hazardous than many others. As a rule I have only to sit at my desk.'

'There you are!' cried Edward Mandeville. He hurried to meet Maisie, and put a glass of champagne into her hand. 'I thought I had lost you.'

'That would have been a terrible shame,' said Maisie. 'Especially as you have brought a drink for me.' She turned to the others. 'Mr Ainsley, Mr De Souza, this is Mr Edward Mandeville of Her Majesty's Indian Civil Service in Bombay. Mr Mandeville, may I present Mr Ainsley and Mr De Souza.'

'Charmed, I'm sure,' said Edward Mandeville, bowing.

'Miss Frobisher, would you show me that painting you mentioned?' asked Mr De Souza. 'It sounds most interesting.'

Maisie tried not to stare. 'Well yes, of course,' she said, offering her arm. 'I shall take my glass with me this time.' She flashed a brilliant smile at Mr Mandeville, and let Mr De Souza lead her off.

'How did you know I wanted to escape?' she murmured, once they were out of earshot.

'A child of five could have seen that,' Mr De Souza murmured back. 'I take it Mr Mandeville is not a friend?'

'Oh no, he is,' said Maisie. 'But he is not a friend I was expecting to see tonight, and I was rather annoyed at being taken possession of.'

'Whereas you don't mind if I do it?'

'I think the painting you wish me to show you is on the opposite side of the room,' Maisie said, to gain time. She willed Miss Jeroboam not to have moved from her seat.

'I thought it might be.' He sounded amused. 'Tell me, Miss Frobisher, haven't I seen you somewhere before?'

'Oh no, I don't think so,' gabbled Maisie. 'I have been in Calcutta for about a week, and I only came to India in October.'

'Oh, then you *are* new,' said Mr De Souza. 'Did you travel from England?'

'Yes, from London.'

'Oh, so you were on the *Britannia*.' He chuckled at Maisie's surprise. 'A merchant such as I knows all the shipping routes, do you see.' Then his face grew serious. 'I don't suppose you were on the same ship as that poor lady explorer? What was the name, now —'

'Jeroboam,' said Maisie, and the word stuck in her throat. 'Miss Charlotte Jeroboam.' She swallowed. She had not expected Leopard to bring up that name so quickly, and here she was leading him towards that very person, who had to remain unrecognised! 'If you don't mind,' she said hurriedly, 'I'd rather not talk about it. Miss Jeroboam was — not a friend, exactly, but someone that I grew to like in our time together on board ship.'

'I am sure she was a charming lady,' said Mr De Souza. 'I am so sorry to have distressed you.'

'It is nothing,' said Maisie, smiling bravely. 'I just wasn't expecting it, and — you caught me off balance.'

'Then I shall strive to bring you back on an even keel, so to speak,' said Mr De Souza, and patted her hand in a fatherly way. 'Now, do you actually have a painting to show me?'

'Not particularly,' said Maisie, recovering some of her composure. 'Perhaps we could take a turn round the room, and you could tell me all about Calcutta. I have not seen half of it yet.'

Mr De Souza laughed. 'I have been here for several years,' he said, 'and I'm not sure that I have, either.'

They wended their way through the room, arm in arm, and Mr De Souza talked of waiting for the ships to enter the harbour at sunrise, his expeditions into the western plains, and the great buildings of the city. 'I know where I've seen you,' he said, stopping suddenly.

'I think you are mistaken,' said Maisie. 'As I said, I have been in Calcutta no more than a week, or two at most —'

'It was at the concert hall!' he exclaimed delightedly. 'I was there on Thursday, for the performance of Sullivan's *Symphony in E*.'

Maisie beamed at him. 'So was I! Did you enjoy it, Mr De Souza?' They resumed their walk, and she realised that they were approaching Miss Jeroboam's corner. Her elaborate red hair showed above the top of her chair, and in the chair next to her lounged Fraser.

Mr De Souza considered. 'It was tolerable,' he said. 'I thought the wind section were perhaps half a beat behind.'

'Oh, did you?' said Maisie, keeping her gaze fixed on him. 'I must admit that I did not notice any discrepancy. Which is your favourite work of Sullivan's? Do you know his comic operas?'

Mr De Souza's answer took him past Miss Jeroboam, and Maisie turned him so that his profile was in clear view. She did not dare to look beyond the man on whose words she hung. 'You do make a good case,' she purred.

'Thank you very much, Miss Frobisher,' said Mr De

Souza, as they strolled into the next part of the room. 'It is a refreshing change to have a cultured conversation with a young lady such as yourself. I declare that most of the young ladies I meet at these — affairs — might as well have a brain full of muslin for all the sense they make.' He glanced at Maisie's dress, and smiled.

'I prefer to keep my muslin where it belongs,' said Maisie, returning his smile. 'I suppose we ought to be getting back to Mr Ainsley — if nothing else, to rescue him from Mr Mandeville.'

'I daresay they are the best of friends by now,' said Mr De Souza, twinkling again. 'But you are right. We must not let Mr Ainsley have too much of a good thing, must we?'

They found Edward Mandeville standing on the edge of a group, sipping his champagne disconsolately. 'I thought you had abandoned me too,' he said. 'That Ainsley fellow said he'd agreed to meet somebody, and shot off a few minutes after you and Mr De Souza.' He frowned. 'Where is everybody, anyway? I haven't even seen the viceroy. And I would have thought that Howarth and Hamilton would return from surveying for this. I mean, the trains are very good.'

'I am so sorry to have monopolised you, Miss Frobisher,' said Mr De Souza, gravely.

'You were gone a long time,' said Edward Mandeville, with a touch of accusation in his voice. 'Eighteen minutes, or thereabouts.'

'Well, Mr Mandeville, I didn't know you were going to be here,' said Maisie, and immediately relented at his hurt expression. 'Why don't you take me for a turn about the room, and perhaps I shall be able to introduce you to the viceroy.'

'What an excellent idea,' said Edward. He offered his arm, and with a sidelong glance of triumph at Mr De Souza, he led Maisie away.

'The only thing with these receptions,' said Maisie, 'is that one does get rather hot.'

Edward laughed. 'Do you think this is hot? Just wait until you have experienced an Indian summer. We were late setting off for the hills, and I have never known anything like it, I can tell you.'

'That is as may be,' said Maisie firmly, steering him towards the French windows. 'However, I am warm now, and fresh air will do me the world of good.' *And it will keep you away from Fraser Hamilton*, she added to herself.

Maisie allowed Edward Mandeville to escort her onto the veranda and find seats for them both. 'I really have missed you, Maisie,' he said, taking her hand. 'That's why I was so glad when the governor said he was sending me over.'

'Oh yes,' said Maisie. 'Why has he sent you here? Are you going to do surveying, too?'

'Oh no, not that,' said Edward. 'The thing is, I can't exactly say. Certainly not before I've seen the viceroy.'

'Oh, but surely you could tell me,' coaxed Maisie. 'I promise I won't tell a soul.'

He looked bashful. 'Oh no, Maisie, I know *you* wouldn't. But one has to be careful. I mean —' He scanned the vicinity elaborately, then lowered his voice. 'I have my suspicions of our new man, Hailey.'

'Oh good heavens,' said Maisie, fighting to keep a straight face. 'Why is that, Edward?'

Edward leaned forward. 'He might be a sort of spy. Not a *bad* spy,' he added, 'although I don't suppose you can ever say a spy is good. I think he's snooping for the viceroy, and not helping us at all.'

'Oh dear,' said Maisie. 'Is that why you have come?'

'Well, it may be related,' said Edward, 'but —'

'Could everyone return to the main hall, please.' Maisie looked up in surprise at Captain James's voice, which had a sharpness she had not heard from him before. 'It is time to say farewell to the viceroy.'

'Gosh, is it?' said Edward, rising. 'It's barely an hour since I got here.'

'As I said earlier, this is not one of the bigger receptions,' said Maisie, giving him her arm. She could tell by the set of Captain James's shoulders and the suppressed energy of his stance that something was wrong. 'Come along, and I shall introduce you to the viceroy before you go.'

They joined the receiving line, and Maisie did as she had promised. 'Your Excellency, this is Mr Edward Mandeville, of the Indian Civil Service in Bombay.'

'Jolly good,' said the viceroy, shaking his hand; but after two pumps his eyes were already on the next guest.

Maisie took Edward outside, and saw him into a rickshaw. 'Won't you come too?' he said, patting the seat beside him. 'You could show me the sights of Calcutta, for it is a beautiful night.'

'I'd love to,' she said, 'but another time, for I have left my shawl inside.'

'I can wait —' he protested, but Maisie was already climbing the steps.

She nodded to the footman, who looked as if he would like to stop her but did not dare, and passed back into the reception room, moving against the tide of departing guests with a bland smile stuck on her face. She scanned the room for signs of trouble, and her eye snagged on a kneeling figure half-hidden by a screen. The trousers suggested uniform, and she hurried towards them.

The man heard her footsteps, straightened, and peeped out. As she had suspected, it was Captain James. 'What has happened?' breathed Maisie, as she approached.

He held up a hand. 'Don't come any closer.'

Footsteps behind the screen, and Fraser looked round it at her. His moustache was still a shock. 'Maisie,' he said, his face expressionless.

'Please tell me what's happened,' said Maisie. 'I'd rather know.'

Fraser's eyes rested on her. 'You knew him, didn't you?'

'Knew who?'

'Ainsley. That's why James has closed the reception. A guest pulled aside a curtain and — and found him. His throat's been cut, and he's dead.'

CHAPTER 10

'I'm so sorry to have to ask you, Miss Frobisher,' said Captain James. 'But you knew him better than anyone else here.' He led Maisie behind the screen, and put aside one of the heavy curtains shielding the window.

Mr Ainsley, swathed in a blanket which covered him up to the chin, huddled awkwardly against the window. His eyes were fixed and staring, his mouth gaped, and his face was splashed with blood.

'Yes, that is Mr Ainsley,' said Maisie, and looked away.

'Thank you,' said Captain James, taking her back round the screen. 'We can't move him until the doctor arrives. He has been summoned, of course. Not that it will do any good for poor Ainsley now.' He rubbed his fingers together absentmindedly, and Maisie gasped as she saw blood. He followed her gaze, and shuddered. 'Damn.'

'I don't understand how this has happened,' said

Maisie. 'I was talking to him not an hour ago.'

'Having one's throat cut does that to a man,' said Fraser grimly. 'It probably took him just minutes to die.'

'But in a room full of people —'

'I know. And Ainsley is covered in blood. How anyone could do this and escape unnoticed —' The inspector shook his head. 'Clearly whoever did it knew what they were doing. Professional, so to speak.' He seemed almost to be talking to himself, then glanced at Maisie. 'You say you were talking to him? How was he?'

'His usual self,' said Maisie, 'as far as I know what that is. I entered the room at perhaps ten minutes past seven, and found him talking to — to Leopard at perhaps twenty past. We exchanged greetings, and then I was called away to —' She regarded him. 'You don't know. Edward Mandeville has turned up.'

'Mandeville? What on earth is he doing here?'

'He didn't say, but it's legitimate. He has a letter from Montgomery. Seal, writing, everything matches. He asked if you were here and I was vague.' Maisie thought. 'So I had to vouch for him, and then we rejoined Mr Ainsley and Leopard. I took Leopard off, to show him to Miss Jeroboam, and when we returned Ainsley was gone. Edward said he'd made an excuse that he had to meet someone.'

'Where is Mandeville now?'

'I put him into a rickshaw,' said Maisie. 'I could tell something was wrong, and I wanted to find out what.'

'Go and see if he's still there,' said Fraser. 'If he is, bring him in. Hopefully he can give us more information about Ainsley's meeting.'

'Is that wise?' asked Captain James.

'Mandeville is an idiot,' the inspector replied, 'but he plays a straight bat.'

'He's probably still outside, waiting for me,' said Maisie. 'While I'm gone, please take that moustache off. And don't ever consider growing one.'

She half-ran into the hallway, slowing to a walk as she passed the viceroy, listening tight-faced to a small voluble man. As she had suspected, the rickshaw was still there, with Edward Mandeville craning his neck to try and see her. She waved and beckoned him. He grinned, jumped out of the rickshaw and ran up the steps, ignoring the protests of the rickshaw driver. His grin faded as he saw her face. 'What's up, Maisie? Couldn't you find it?'

'Find what? Oh, never mind that. Edward, something terrible has happened and we need information.'

'What do you mean?'

Maisie linked her arm through his and steered him into the hall, past the viceroy, and into the reception room. 'I have found Mr Mandeville,' she called into the apparently empty space.

Fraser, now moustacheless, emerged from behind the screen. 'Good.'

'Hamilton!' exclaimed Edward Mandeville. 'I thought you were surveying.' He turned to Maisie. 'Did *you* know he was here?'

'Mandeville, this is important,' said Fraser, walking over. 'You must tell me everything you can about the time you spent with Mr Ainsley tonight.' He rubbed his upper lip, which was slightly pink.

'What? Why?' Edward stared at him. 'What does it have to do with you? And where did you get that suit? Been splashing out, have we?'

Maisie patted his arm. 'Just — just do as he says, Edward.'

They looked up at the sound of the door opening. Lord Strathcairn strode towards them. 'Damn dignitaries,' he said, 'I thought he'd never go. What's the situation, James?'

'The doctor is coming, but Ainsley's past help,' said the captain. 'This man Mandeville may have been one of the last to see him alive.'

'Do you mean he's dead?' cried Edward. 'But he can't be.'

'He is,' said Fraser, 'and that's why you must talk to me.'

'You mean . . . it's murder?' Maisie could feel the arm she still held begin to tremble.

'I think we can safely say that,' remarked the viceroy. 'So I suggest you do as the inspector says, and tell him everything you know.'

'The inspector?' Edward Mandeville stared at Fraser, and gradually comprehension dawned. 'So you're not a Civil Service man?'

'No,' said Fraser.

'And you were never stationed in Madras?'

'Again, no.' Fraser turned to the captain. 'Is there a room I can use, James?'

'The blue anteroom is out of the way,' replied the

captain.

'Excellent. Follow me.'

A servant appeared at the door. 'The doctor is here, Your Excellency.'

'Show him in,' said Lord Strathcairn. 'James, Hamilton, I shall be in my study. Let me know any news.' He eyed Maisie. 'Miss Frobisher, I suggest that you return to your hotel.'

'Oh, but —' Everyone looked at Edward, and he blushed. 'Maisie, would you mind staying with me? When Hamilton talks to me, I mean.' He grew even redder. 'I get terribly forgetful, and you could help me fill in the detail.'

Lord Strathcairn studied the young man, barely hiding his contempt. 'That might not be such a bad idea, if Miss Frobisher is agreeable.'

'Oh, thank you, sir — I mean Your Excellency,' said Edward, half-bowing. 'I had no idea Hamilton was a policeman, you see. It's all rather a shock, especially given the reason I'm here.'

'That's a good point,' said Fraser. 'Why *are* you here?'

'I was only supposed to tell the viceroy,' said Edward. 'But as he's here, it can't do any harm. Lord Montgomery sent me to bring you back. And he said I wasn't to take no for an answer.'

***

Edward Mandeville had little information to impart. Miss Frobisher had introduced him to Mr Ainsley and another gentleman, and they had spoken briefly before the other chap — Mr Souza was it? — had taken Maisie to look at some picture. 'I rather thought he had designs on you,' he said, with a note of reproach in his voice. 'I hope he behaved himself.'

'Of course he did,' snapped Maisie. 'What did you and Mr Ainsley talk about while we were gone?'

'Nothing much,' said Edward. 'He said he was a merchant, which I know nothing of, and he didn't ask me anything about the Service. Clearly we had nothing in common. I'm not good at small talk with people I don't know.'

'And you were angry that another chap had poached Miss Frobisher,' commented Fraser.

'I say, old man, that's hardly fair,' protested Edward.

'But is it true?' Fraser regarded him steadily.

Edward Mandeville fidgeted. 'I suppose it is. Don't write that, please.'

Fraser laid down his pen. 'So did you leave Mr Ainsley, or did Mr Ainsley leave you?'

'He left me,' said Edward. 'And I must say that he did it rather rudely. He looked very obviously at his watch, said "Is that the time? Excuse me, but I have a rendezvous," and strolled off.'

'And how long did you talk before he left?'

Edward Mandeville considered. 'Not more than three minutes, I would say. Wait —' He thought for a moment. 'I checked my watch when Miss Frobisher returned, and saw that she had been gone for eighteen minutes.'

'And what time was it then?' asked Fraser, pen poised.

'It was ten minutes to eight,' said Edward. 'So Ainsley and I were talking at just after half past seven, and I must have spent a good fifteen minutes on my own.'

'Indeed.' The pen scratched. 'Thank you, Mandeville, that is helpful. And did you stay in the same place while Miss Frobisher was gone?'

Edward looked shamefaced. 'No. I, um, wandered about a bit to see if I could find anyone else I knew.' He shot an accusing glance at Fraser. 'Where were you hiding?'

Fraser regarded him coolly. 'I was busy.'

Edward Mandeville cleared his throat. 'After a few minutes I gave up, got another glass of champagne, and decided to return to my original spot, in case Miss Frobisher came back. Which she did.' His voice held a note of triumph.

'Miss Frobisher, can you confirm that, as far as you're aware, Mr Mandeville's account is true and correct?' Fraser enquired, his eyebrows raised.

'Yes, Inspector Hamilton,' said Maisie. 'As far as I know, that is correct.'

'Excellent,' said Fraser, capping his pen. 'Mandeville, where can I reach you? We may have more questions for you.'

'I am staying at the Hotel Superior,' said Edward, rising. 'But I daresay I shall be at Government House often enough, conducting my business.' He studied Fraser. 'Does the governor know you're a policeman?'

'Thank you for your time, Mr Mandeville,' said Fraser. 'I'll show you out.'

Edward lingered on the threshold. 'Won't you share a carriage, Miss Frobisher?' he said, plaintively.

'I'm afraid that won't be possible,' said Fraser. 'I must

take a statement from Miss Frobisher too before she leaves.'

'Oh!' Edward Mandeville stepped forward. 'A word in your ear, Hamilton.' He took Fraser aside and muttered something. 'You know where to find me now too, Miss Frobisher. I hope to see you again very soon.' He bowed to her, and took his leave.

'What did he say to you?' asked Maisie, once the front door was closed.

Fraser smiled. 'He cautioned me to treat you with the delicacy due to a young lady of your station. My new position and my dress clothes may have unnerved him.'

'It's as well he didn't see the moustache,' commented Maisie. She reached up and stroked his upper lip, now only faintly pink, then leaned her head on his chest. 'What on earth will happen next?'

Fraser put his arms around her, and held her close. 'A murder investigation,' he said. 'On top of all the other things, a murder investigation.'

CHAPTER 11

When Maisie arrived at Government House the next morning she was shown straight to the blue anteroom. Whereas before it had resembled a small parlour, the comfortable sofas and armchairs had been removed, and a desk brought in. Already it was covered in papers, and behind it sat Fraser, frowning at a file.

'Good morning, Maisie,' he said. He already sounded weary, despite the early hour. 'I don't suppose you have any new insights for me?'

'Unfortunately not,' said Maisie. 'Have you any leads?'

Fraser shook his head. 'I have the basics; a list of everyone invited to the reception, intelligence of who came, and, thanks to James's quick thinking, a list of everyone who left at the end of the reception.'

'And are there any discrepancies?' asked Maisie.

'Just two,' said Fraser. 'But both of those people left

while Ainsley was still alive.' He sighed. 'I entirely understand why the viceroy wanted everyone to leave as quickly as possible. After all, with a murderer in our midst, who's to say that he might not have tried again that evening? But it also means that the murderer will have had the chance to remove any traces of the crime by the time we get to him or her.'

'And dispose of the weapon,' said Maisie.

'Oh, they did that at the scene,' said Fraser. 'We found it in Ainsley's pocket. A cut-throat razor. And no, sadly it didn't have its owner's initials engraved on it. It is a cheap razor such as could be bought in any shop in India.'

'Does that mean it was planned?' said Maisie. 'If it had been a penknife, say, it might have been a spur-of-the-moment thing. Who brings a cut-throat razor to a reception?'

'Someone who is prepared to kill,' said Fraser.

They were interrupted by a tap at the door. 'Mrs Carter is here, sir,' said the servant.

'Thank you,' said Fraser. 'Please wait three minutes, then show her in.'

'Of course, sir.' The servant bowed and withdrew.

Fraser made a perfunctory attempt to tidy his papers, then pushed his hair back from his forehead. 'I daresay this will be difficult,' he said. 'The viceroy told me that she thought very highly of Ainsley.' His focus returned to Maisie. 'Please will you do something for me?'

'Yes, what is it?' said Maisie.

'Would you talk to Miss Jeroboam? Ask her what she saw last night, if anything. With all this going on, I've barely spoken to her.'

'About the murder, you mean?'

'About the murder, about Leopard, about anything.' Fraser looked despondent. 'I feel as if I'm struggling to keep my head above water.' Then he gasped. 'Please don't repeat that to her! She'll think I'm poking fun.'

Maisie allowed herself a smile. 'Quite possibly. Yes, I'll go now.' She paused. 'Will Mrs Carter be with you for long?'

Fraser shrugged. 'I really don't know.' He squared off the papers on his desk as Maisie left; and mindful of Mrs Carter's friendship with Ainsley, Maisie took a roundabout route to Miss Jeroboam's apartments.

She found Charlotte Jeroboam frowning over a sheet of paper, pen poised. 'Oh hello, Maisie,' she said, screwing the lid onto her pen and laying it down. 'What brings you here? Have you come to discuss the nice men you met last night?'

'Hardly,' said Maisie. 'Are you aware of what happened last night at the reception? Has anyone told you?'

Miss Jeroboam shook her head. 'I gathered from its hasty conclusion that something had happened, but I was got out of the way by a servant.' Her eyes narrowed. 'What did happen?'

'Someone was murdered,' said Maisie.

Miss Jeroboam looked first surprised, then amused. 'Well, unless it was Inspector Hamilton, I am in the clear,' she said. 'He sat with me all night until he handed me over to a servant.'

'That isn't quite what I meant,' said Maisie. 'Do you

recall seeing an elderly man, of medium height and broad shoulders, somewhat yellow in complexion and with dark eyes?'

Miss Jeroboam thought for a moment, then shook her head. 'I might have done; but if I did I took no notice of such a person. I was too busy watching for you and your escort.'

Maisie decided to change tack. 'And you saw us?'

Miss Jeroboam laughed. 'Of course I saw you! How could I not? You paraded that poor man in front of me as though he were a prize bull and I an avaricious farmer.'

'And…?' prompted Maisie. 'Was he the man who recruited you in London?'

'He was very like,' said Miss Jeroboam. 'Of the right build and complexion, certainly. And of course one has to account for the fact that when we met in London, he was not in evening dress. But in bearing, manner, and voice, he was not the same at all.'

'Oh,' said Maisie. 'But a walk, a manner, or a voice could be assumed.'

'They could,' said Miss Jeroboam. 'But the man I spoke to in London had a high, harsh voice, and when he smiled he looked completely different from the man you escorted around the room last night. Even his teeth were not the same.'

'What did he call himself?' asked Maisie. She felt as if she were clutching at straws to keep open the convenient possibility that Leopard had recruited Miss Jeroboam.

'I've been thinking about that,' said Miss Jeroboam, tapping the sheet of paper before her. It contained a few lines written in her flowing script; but much of it was crossed through. 'I have been trying to recall as much as I can and write it down, since my memory plays tricks with me. That man's name is one of the things which is gone. I remember that it was an unusual name —'

'Was it Leopard?'

Miss Jeroboam stared at her. '*What?* Did you say leopard?' She giggled. 'It definitely wasn't that.' Then she looked thoughtful. 'Now you've said that, though, it seems familiar. I shall write it on my sheet of paper, and see if any answers come to me.'

'Thank you,' said Maisie. She made to get up, then saw the hurt in Miss Jeroboam's eyes and sat back down. 'So tell me about the rest of the evening. Did you like the inspector's moustache?'

Miss Jeroboam giggled again. 'I can't say that I did,' she replied. 'But his suit was beyond reproach, of course, and he was good company. He told me the name of everyone he knew in the room, and we made up stories about those he didn't. Oh, and he made sure I was supplied with champagne and treats. I felt as if I were still a lady, and rather a fine one at that.' She looked pensive for a while, then smiled at Maisie. 'If he treats you in the same way, perhaps I can understand what you see in him.'

'I'm not sure he is half so nice to me,' Maisie replied. 'We bicker and tease each other much of the time. Nevertheless, we get along very well.'

'"Get along very well,"' mocked Miss Jeroboam. 'I've seen how you look at each other. I only hope that I shall be able to buy a hat of suitable magnificence when the time comes.' She thought for a moment. 'Did the Merritts ever get married?'

'Oh yes,' said Maisie. 'I think they have just returned from honeymoon.'

'Lucky things,' said Miss Jeroboam, her face wistful. Then she caught Maisie watching her, and laughed merrily. 'Now I remember you had not one companion, but two! Who was the awkward young chap I saw you with? You didn't seem exactly pleased to be in his company.'

'I wasn't, really,' said Maisie. 'He did get in the way so. Mr Mandeville, whom I met in Bombay. He fastened on to me as I was the sole person he knew.'

'Oh, it is so inconvenient when that happens,' said Miss Jeroboam. 'Has he no redeeming features whatsoever?'

'The only one I can think of at present is that he is a fan of yours,' said Maisie, laughing.

Miss Jeroboam frowned. 'He doesn't know I'm here, does he?'

'No, not at all,' Maisie assured her. 'But when I chatted to him at dinner in Bombay he had read your papers, and was looking forward very much to meeting you.'

'Oh well,' said Miss Jeroboam. 'Perhaps one day.' She yawned elaborately. 'Maisie Frobisher, you have tired me out yet again.' She pushed the paper and pen away and rested her head against the antimacassar. 'Perhaps that man's name will come to me in a dream,' she remarked, closing her eyes. 'If it does, I shall be sure to let you know.'

Maisie went quietly from the room and made her way back to the blue anteroom. However, as she approached it she heard a woman's voice speaking. *Surely that can't be Mrs Carter*, she thought. The voice was low and hoarse, as if speaking were painful. 'I shall never forgive myself,' the woman said. 'I thought I was giving him a treat, almost — a glittering reception, with little to do — and instead I sent him to his death!' The last word dissolved into a sob, and Maisie crept quietly away.

She took refuge on the veranda, where a servant brought her a glass of lemonade and that day's paper. Maisie scanned the first few pages for any mention of Ainsley's death, and finding nothing, sat back and thought. Who could have wanted to kill Ainsley? Who had known his motive for being there? And if Leopard was not the man Miss Jeroboam had met in London, then who was? The three questions chased each other around Maisie's brain till she felt giddy. She rubbed her forehead to erase them, and leafed through the paper for inspiration; but all she found was local information, news of a very minor nature, and ink-stained hands.

CHAPTER 12

Maisie was roused from her reverie by a discreet cough. 'Excuse me, madam,' said the servant, 'I have a letter for you.'

'A letter? For me?' Maisie reached out her hand then stopped, conscious of her inky fingers. 'Please excuse me for a moment, I must wash my hands.'

Maisie washed her hands thoroughly in the small cloakroom off the hall. Who would send a letter for her to Government House? 'I thought I gave everyone my new address,' she murmured, putting her gloves on. Clearly the only way to discover who had sent the letter was to read it.

When she returned to the veranda the servant was waiting, rocking on the balls of his feet, her letter bobbing behind his back. He saw her, and held it out with a bow. Maisie took the letter, sat down, and, since the servant was still hovering, looked hard at him until he retreated.

Miss Maisie Frobisher, care of Government House, Calcutta. The handwriting was neat, perhaps a little laborious, and some of the letters were unusually formed. It was not a hand she had seen before. Inside was a note and two invitations; one addressed to her, and one blank.

Dear Miss Frobisher,

It was a pleasure to meet you last night at the Viceroy's reception, and I am only sorry that it ended so soon.

I hope you will not think me forward, but I am hosting a little gathering on Friday evening. Nothing too formal — merely a buffet with music — but it would be very nice to see you.

I understand you may be reluctant to come alone to the house of a comparative stranger. Therefore, perhaps you would like to invite your friend Mr Mandeville as your guardian and protector. I dare say that, should we desire a little private conversation, it can be managed.

Yours in anticipation,
Anton De Souza

Maisie stared at the letter till the words made no sense.

The servant approached. 'Does madam need to send an answer? I can bring pen and paper, if madam desires them.'

'I, um, I'm not sure,' said Maisie. 'I shall speak to someone before I decide.'

The servant bowed. 'Very wise, madam.' He took two steps back, and waited.

A few minutes later Maisie found herself standing

outside the blue anteroom, but she could not have said how she had got there. She could still hear voices — now raised voices — but paid no heed, and knocked.

'Come!' Fraser's tone was clipped, abrupt, but he smiled when he saw her. 'Ah, it's you, Maisie. What did Miss Jeroboam say?'

'Miss Jeroboam? Oh yes.' Her visit to Miss Jeroboam's room seemed a lifetime ago. 'She doesn't think it's the same man, though very like. But that isn't what I came to talk to you about.'

'Well, take a seat, and perhaps you could help us settle an argument.' Fraser's glance slid towards Mrs Carter, who was sitting very upright on the chair opposite. 'Mrs Carter and I have a difference of opinion over whether to bring Leopard in for questioning.'

'Yes, we do,' said Mrs Carter. 'If that man isn't involved in my friend's murder, I'll —'

'Whereas I don't see how on earth Mr De Souza could have murdered Ainsley, seeing as he was strolling around with you for most of the evening.' Fraser's voice was light but he held himself stiffly, as if holding in his anger.

'The sooner that man is brought in and cross-examined, the sooner we shall get to the bottom of this,' said Mrs Carter. She held her large bag on her lap, and her knuckles were white.

'I need to show you both something,' Maisie said, and laid her letter on the desk. 'I received this not ten minutes ago, and it is from Anton De Souza.'

The inspector took up the letter, studied it, then handed it to Mrs Carter. 'Well done, Maisie,' he said. 'Your charm works yet again. But I don't think you should go, and certainly not with Mandeville. He is as much use as a parasol in a monsoon.'

'And why shouldn't Miss Frobisher go?' demanded Mrs Carter. 'You've just been saying that you don't think De Souza had anything to do with Ainsley's murder, so where's the harm in her going?'

Maisie looked from one to the other. 'If I do go, Fraser, whom do you propose I take instead of Mr Mandeville?'

Fraser's eyebrows shot up. 'Why, me, of course.'

Mrs Carter snorted. 'Didn't you get knocked out the last time you tried to protect Miss Frobisher?'

Fraser scowled at her, then turned to Maisie. 'It isn't up to either of us. What do you want to do?'

Maisie studied her clasped hands. 'I'm not sure,' she said. 'I don't think anything will happen to me there, if that's what you're afraid of. This probably sounds ridiculous, but he seemed too — nice — to do anything like that.'

'Nice!' cried Mrs Carter. 'That man, nice?'

Maisie sighed. 'If you two can't agree, and I don't know, there is only one thing for it,' she said. 'The viceroy must decide.'

***

Lord Strathcairn regarded Maisie over the top of his spectacles, then took them off. 'I won't ask what you said to the man, Miss Frobisher.' His smile was bleak as a winter day. He tapped the letter with the arm of his spectacles. 'Whatever it was, it seems to have worked.'

'I was merely pleasant,' said Maisie, feeling rather

injured.

'I meant it as praise, Miss Frobisher,' remarked the viceroy. 'Are you minded to go?'

'I'm not sure,' said Maisie. 'And Mrs Carter and the inspector can't agree.'

The viceroy glanced to her left, where Fraser and Mrs Carter sat stiffly on adjacent chairs. 'That's the problem with decisions by committee,' he said. 'They happen so rarely.' He focused on Maisie again. 'Do you think this Mandeville fellow can do a reasonable job of looking after you?'

'I am sure that he would be able to protect me, if that were needed,' Maisie said. 'I am perhaps more concerned that he might make a faux pas, or stick to me so closely that the event will be useless.'

'I see.' Lord Strathcairn's eyes rested on Fraser. 'Hamilton, you said Mandeville was an honest chap, didn't you?'

'As far as I know,' said Fraser. 'We don't like each other particularly, but I have always had fair dealings with him.'

'Then the way forward is clear,' said the viceroy. 'We must get him on board and make him understand what his role is in the matter.'

'But sir —'

'Your Excellency,' said the viceroy, with a gleam in his eye.

'I beg your pardon, Your Excellency.' Fraser twitched in his seat. 'I just don't think he's capable.'

The viceroy raised his eyebrows. 'All he needs to do is escort Miss Frobisher, look smart, speak when he's spoken to, and get out of the way as required.' He studied Fraser. 'I suppose you think you'd do a better job of it.'

'He can't,' said Mrs Carter flatly. 'There is too much risk that De Souza will recognise him from the cathedral, where Inspector Hamilton shadowed him.'

'That settles it,' said Lord Strathcairn, returning the letter to Maisie. 'Miss Frobisher, if you have no objections, please write to Mr De Souza accepting his kind invitation, and invite Mr Mandeville as your escort.' Maisie heard an exasperated noise behind her. 'Inspector Hamilton, the murder investigation must be your top priority. Please attend me at eight o'clock tomorrow morning to report your progress so far.' The viceroy put his spectacles back on. 'Anything else?'

Maisie shook her head. 'That is all, Your Excellency.'

'Then I shall let you get on,' the viceroy said. 'Good day to you.'

The trio walked down the corridor in silence. Finally Mrs Carter sighed. 'I got some of what I wanted,' she said. 'Miss Frobisher, if there is anything I can do to help —' She opened her bag and gave Maisie a card from her case. 'This is where you can find me.'

'Thank you,' said Maisie, putting it in her own bag. 'I may be in touch.'

Mrs Carter nodded briskly. 'See that you are.' She walked away as straight-backed as ever; but her shoulders drooped.

Fraser muttered something, and Maisie turned to him. 'I'm sorry, I didn't catch that.'

'I'm not happy about this,' he said, glaring at her. 'You

knew I didn't want you to go, and yet you've agreed to it, and with that ass Mandeville of all people. Is my judgement worth nothing?' Suddenly the fierceness of his expression dissolved, and he looked stricken.

'Oh Fraser, I would much rather go with you,' said Maisie, laying a hand on his arm. 'But I can't. If Leopard recognises you, and you're with me, that puts us both in danger.'

'I know,' said Fraser. He sighed. 'That doesn't make it any easier, though.'

'And the viceroy's right,' said Maisie. 'You're needed at the murder investigation. Edward Mandeville is just a convenient gentleman to make use of.'

'I hope you won't put that in your invitation,' said Fraser; but he smiled.

'That's better,' said Maisie, and kissed him. 'I promise to behave impeccably.'

'I'll believe that when I see it,' said Fraser, and kissed her back. 'Now go and write your letters. Some of us have work to do.'

Maisie returned to the veranda, asked for pen and paper, and set to work. But as she thought, and tapped her pen on her teeth, she recalled Fraser's anger, and his injured look. 'It isn't my fault,' she said to herself, as she wrote Edward Mandeville's name on the blank invitation. 'I can hardly help the way things have turned out.' And as she ruminated on the best form of words for the accompanying note, resentment prickled at her like a pin left in a new dress. *Who is he to decide what I do?* she thought, laying her pen down in case she made a blot through bad temper. *I am my own woman, and I shall do what I think is right.* She nodded firmly, and in her indignation dashed off a missive which was somewhat warmer than her original intention. She read it, grimaced, then shrugged and addressed the envelope. *Let him make what he likes of it,* she thought. *If I cannot manage Edward Mandeville, I am in a sorry state indeed.*

CHAPTER 13

Edward Mandeville's response arrived in the following day's lunchtime post.

Dear Maisie,
Thank you so much for your kind invitation — I say yours, because the card is in your handwriting. I would be delighted to accompany you to Mr De Souza's house on Friday.
Might we meet before then, though? I would welcome the opportunity to talk to you, given recent events.
Yours ever,
Edward

He is warming up, thought Maisie. Part of her was a little mortified that perhaps she had been over-friendly, but the note's success was clear. *It is what it is*, she told herself.

The same post brought a note in Miss Jeroboam's flowing hand.

Dear Maisie,

My sources have revealed that you are planning to visit Leopard in his lair. Could you call on me first? I have cudgelled my poor brain and beaten out a piece of information which may prove useful.

Sincerely,
Charlotte

Maisie glanced at her watch. Almost two o'clock. 'Perfect,' she said, and caught up her gloves and bag.

Charlotte Jeroboam received her with a smile. 'I see my note has had the desired effect,' she said. 'However, don't get too excited.' She waved her hand at the side table, on which lay a few sheets of paper filled with writing. Maisie started towards it, but Miss Jeroboam held up a hand. 'Wait! First, tell me: are the rumours true? Are you really going to Leopard's house?'

Maisie sat down, and faced her. 'Yes, I am. It is an unexpected opportunity to learn more about him. And if he has anything to do with Mr Ainsley's murder, perhaps I shall discover a clue.'

'I see,' said Miss Jeroboam. She frowned. 'You're not going alone, are you?'

'No, of course not,' said Maisie. 'A young man of my acquaintance is taking me.'

'A young man of your acquaintance!' Miss Jeroboam

laughed. 'That's a funny way to describe Inspector Hamilton.'

'It would be, if it were him,' Maisie answered. 'I am taking someone else.'

'Are you?' Miss Jeroboam raised her eyebrows. 'What does the inspector have to say about that?'

'He understands that it is necessary,' said Maisie.

'Such a diplomatic answer,' said Miss Jeroboam. 'You have clearly been here a little too long.' She studied Maisie. 'Before I share my knowledge, let me offer a word of wisdom.' She paused, considering her words. 'Don't let the thrill of the chase overtake your whole life.'

Maisie stared at her. 'What do you mean by that?'

'What I say,' replied Miss Jeroboam. 'Perhaps if I had taken a step back in London, and thought about what I was undertaking, I would have made a different decision — and then I would not be stuck in an invalid's room facilitating someone else's adventure.' Her words were bitter, but her tone was not. 'Anyway, let me show you what I have remembered. It isn't much; but it may help.' She got up and went to the table. 'Come, sit beside me,' she said, and coughed. 'Let me find the right sheet,' she muttered, and leafed through the small pile. 'Here.' She underlined a phrase with her finger. Above and below were deletions, but that phrase was clear.

'*The flamingo flies high*,' read Maisie. 'What does it mean?'

'It is a phrase I was supposed to say,' replied Miss Jeroboam. 'A sort of password. I was to spend a couple of days in Bombay, accept any invitations I was offered, and my contact would find me at one of those. He would say something about a bird, and that would be my reply.'

'Oh!' Maisie looked at the paper. 'Are you absolutely sure?'

'As sure as I can be, given my patchy memory.' Miss Jeroboam tapped her forehead. 'You may read the rest of the sheets if you like, though I doubt you will get much from them. It is a crazy patchwork sewn together all wrong, but perhaps you can make more sense of it than I.'

Maisie scanned through the sheets. Miss Jeroboam was right. More was crossed out than left unamended, and she could make neither head nor tail of the rest.

'I'm sorry,' said Miss Jeroboam, looking upset. 'I wrote down everything that came to me, in the hope that some would be useful.' Her mouth twisted, and she hid her face in her hands. 'Everything is so hard,' she muttered. 'All the things that were easy, and so much has gone.'

Maisie moved her chair closer and put an arm around Charlotte Jeroboam's shoulders, which made her cry in earnest. Maisie gave her a handkerchief, and held her until her sobs eased. 'I am so sorry,' she said, wiping her eyes and blowing her nose. 'I never cry. I don't know what has come over me.'

'You have every reason to be upset,' said Maisie. 'Perhaps you needed to cry.'

'Perhaps.' Miss Jeroboam grimaced and put Maisie's handkerchief in her pocket. 'I shall make sure this is laundered and returned to you,' she said briskly. 'But remember what I said. Not just about the flamingo; about you.' She sighed. 'What will you do when you leave me?'

'I hadn't thought that far,' said Maisie.

'In that case,' said Miss Jeroboam, 'I suggest that you go and visit the inspector, and see how he is getting on.'

'Are you worried that his nose is out of joint?' laughed Maisie.

Miss Jeroboam smiled. 'He visited me yesterday afternoon, which is how I came to learn of your little expedition. If that doesn't show that he is in a bad way, I don't know what does.'

Again Maisie felt that stab of annoyance. Fraser had discussed her affairs with someone else, even though that someone else was her friend. 'Very well, I shall go and see him,' she said, rising.

'Don't tell him I said anything.'

'I won't,' said Maisie. 'And if I don't see you before Friday, I shall come and tell you all about it afterwards.'

'I shall look forward to it,' said Miss Jeroboam. 'Safe travels, Miss Frobisher.'

***

When Maisie reached the blue anteroom she heard voices within. One was Fraser's, the other she didn't recognise. A servant was on duty nearby. 'Do you know when the inspector will be free?' asked Maisie.

'He said he wasn't to be disturbed until half past three, madam.'

Maisie looked at her watch. Half an hour to wait. 'In that case, when the inspector is unoccupied, could you tell him that I would like to speak with him. I shall be on the veranda.'

The servant came to find her at a quarter to four. 'The

inspector can see you now, madam.'

How ridiculous, thought Maisie. *Not two weeks ago we were talking of returning to England to marry, and here we are communicating through a servant.* 'Thank you,' she said, rather shortly, and took her time gathering up her belongings and following the servant back through Government House.

As usual, Fraser was behind his desk and a heap of papers, which seemed to have grown since her last visit. 'What brings you here, Maisie?'

'I came to see how you were getting on,' said Maisie, sitting down.

'Oh.' He looked at his desk. 'I have spent yesterday afternoon and all day today interviewing as many guests from the viceroy's reception as I can get hold of, and frankly I'm not much the wiser. No one remembers seeing Ainsley, no one recalls anyone acting suspiciously.' He snorted. 'Ainsley's training in unobtrusiveness served him badly in this instance. Not that I'll be telling Mrs Carter that.'

'Oh yes, I must call on Mrs Carter,' said Maisie. 'Thank you for reminding me.'

'What it is to be so busy,' Fraser commented. 'Have you sent Mandeville his tea-party invitation yet?'

'Yes, I have,' said Maisie, 'and he has accepted.' She debated whether to tell Fraser that he had asked to meet her beforehand, and decided that, given his current mood, that would be unwise.

'No doubt he is delighted,' said Fraser. 'I only hope he doesn't mess it up.'

'He won't,' said Maisie. 'I'll make sure of that.'

'Will you, now.' Fraser's expression suggested he had detected an unpleasant smell.

'Yes, I shall,' said Maisie. 'We are meeting beforehand so that Edward knows everything he needs to. Miss Jeroboam has remembered something which may be useful to us, and I shall brief him on the matter.'

'Has she?' Fraser leaned forward. 'What is it?'

'I don't think you need to know,' said Maisie.

The inspector gasped. 'It's like that, is it?' he cried.

'It doesn't have to be,' said Maisie. 'But if you persist in being resentful and mistrustful, then I don't see why I should tell you anything. Good day.' She rose, swept from the room, and asked the servant to summon a carriage for her.

Maisie arrived back at the hotel in time for afternoon tea, but chose to take it in her room. *In my present mood I am no fit company for anyone*, she thought. *I should probably growl at them.* The thought of herself snapping at a well-meaning table-mate made her giggle, and dissipated some of her ill-humour.

Two cups of strong Assam tea and a selection of sandwiches and cakes finished the job, and Maisie sat down to reply to Edward Mandeville's note feeling considerably better.

Dear Edward,

I am so glad that you can come, and many thanks for your prompt reply.

I would also like to speak with you before the event. I

imagine you are busy during the day, so perhaps we could meet for dinner tomorrow? I can recommend the Punjabi as a nice quiet restaurant, with excellent food, where we may talk in private.

Yours,
Maisie

Maisie read the letter through. Was inviting him to take her to dinner the right thing to do? *Would Fraser do the same thing in my position,* she asked herself. *Yes, I am sure he would. And if he did, I would understand.* She blotted the letter, sealed it in an envelope, and rang for the page to take it to the post.

CHAPTER 14

Maisie rang the Carters' doorbell, and shifted from foot to foot as she waited. It was not the grandeur of the residence that discomfited her, though they lived in a smart bungalow on one of the best roads in Calcutta. She pulled out Mrs Carter's card and studied it. *Estella Carter*, it said, *Advisor*. That one ambiguous word made Maisie wonder what Mrs Carter had in store for her.

The door opened and a servant looked her up and down. 'Miss Frobisher?'

Maisie gaped. 'How do you know who I am?'

The servant smiled. 'Mrs Carter said I was to expect you, and gave me a description. This way, please.'

The inside of the bungalow was well but plainly furnished; not in what Maisie would have judged to be Mrs Carter's style. The servant tapped at a closed door, then entered. 'Miss Frobisher has arrived, ma'am.'

'Excellent. Show her in.' It was Mrs Carter's voice, in its most businesslike form.

Mrs Carter was sitting in an armchair, an embroidery hoop on her lap. 'Do sit, dear,' she said, indicating the closest armchair.

'Thank you,' said Maisie, taking a seat. 'This is nice.'

Mrs Carter blinked. 'It isn't what I would choose,' she replied. 'However, as we have borrowed it, one can't complain.' She addressed the servant. 'Please could you bring us tea.'

She placed her hoop on the table next to her. 'I expect you're wondering why I invited you to visit, Miss Frobisher. After all, we were very satisfied with the arrangements made for Friday.' She paused, her eyes on Maisie's face.

Maisie smiled. 'I'm not sure satisfied is exactly the word I would use, Mrs Carter.'

'No. I for one would prefer to drag Leopard into a police station and interrogate him myself.' Maisie imagined Mrs Carter stabbing a needle through her embroidery. 'However, that is not why I have invited you here. While you have been assigned a protector, I personally would not trust any man to look after me.' She rose and went to a cupboard in the corner of the room, from which she produced a small reticule.

'I do have the gun which Lord Montgomery gave me,' ventured Maisie.

Mrs Carter stared at her, then dissolved into peals of laughter. 'My dear, you can't possibly go into Leopard's house with a gun! What if someone finds it? You might as well announce that you don't trust your host. Unless you would rather he thought you were planning to shoot him. Better this way.' She put the reticule into Maisie's hands. 'Unpack it, please.'

Maisie delved into the reticule, and brought out a small pouch. Inside was a sewing kit; needles threaded with fine silk, a card of pins, and a tiny pair of scissors. 'I'm really not sure —'

'I find a jab with a needle or a pin can work wonders in a tight spot,' said Mrs Carter. 'The pins are fairly harmless. The needle with yellow thread, however, has been dipped in a muscle relaxant. It will have an effect within a few minutes, and providing you are in a one-on-one situation, you should be able to escape. The needle with red thread —' She looked at Maisie. 'Don't use that one unless you absolutely have to. It is poisonous. Oh, and if you need something more straightforward, the scissors are deadly sharp.'

'I see,' said Maisie, closing the pouch hastily and returning it to the reticule. Next she pulled out a small lidded cylinder. 'Should I open it?' she asked, looking at it doubtfully.

Mrs Carter laughed. 'Don't worry, the worst you would get from that is a sneezing fit, since it contains pepper. Useful for seasoning food, but also handy for throwing into an adversary's face, and in particular the eyes. That will buy you at least an extra minute.'

Maisie put it back, and drew out a pen. 'What does this do?' she asked.

'Well, it writes,' said Mrs Carter. 'But it does so in

invisible ink. Easy to write a letter and include a private message between the lines, or in the margins. Obviously you will need to carry a normal pen as well.'

Finally Maisie extracted a small packet of hairpins. 'I assume these aren't to keep my hair tidy.'

Mrs Carter regarded her critically. 'You do have several stray wisps, Miss Frobisher, which would certainly annoy me. However, these are for picking locks.'

'But I don't know how —'

'Which is one of the reasons why I invited you to call on me,' said Mrs Carter firmly. 'I shall ask Avik to fetch some locks of standard make, and more hairpins, and we shall see how you get on. After that, we shall move to hands-on self-defence.'

Maisie eyed her hostess's plump form. 'Oh, but I couldn't —'

Mrs Carter giggled. 'Not on me, you goose! No, I shall demonstrate on Avik, and then you may have a go. Don't worry, we won't hurt him.' A tap at the door signalled the entry of Avik, with a tea tray. 'We shan't hurt you, Avik, shall we?'

'I doubt it, madam,' said Avik, gravely. 'And in return, I shall not hurt either of you.'

'Agreed,' said Mrs Carter. 'Now if you could bring us those locks and a packet of pins, we shall begin our first lesson.'

***

'This is delightful,' said Edward Mandeville, gazing round the quiet restaurant with what Maisie felt was perhaps an excess of enthusiasm.

He had called for her at exactly the time he had said he would. In truth, Maisie would have preferred him to be late, since she had left Mrs Carter's house in a state of dishevelled exhaustion. Her muscles had never worked so hard before, and her brain was scarcely in better shape.

At the end of two hours Mrs Carter had pronounced herself satisfied with Maisie's progress. 'Not at all bad for a first go, my dear,' she said, beaming. She herself had barely a hair out of place, and looked as if she had taken a slow stroll around her garden.

'How do you do it?' Maisie had gasped.

'Practice, my dear.' Mrs Carter poured Maisie a cup of fresh tea, and one for herself. 'I try my skills once a week without fail. If no one else is available, Randolph and I practise on each other.'

'I see,' said Maisie, trying not to imagine the spectacle, and completely failing. She suspected Randolph Carter would get the worst of it.

'Do stop that, dear, I can see you thinking,' said Mrs Carter. 'Do you feel a little more ready for Friday?'

Maisie smiled. 'Yes, I do. The difficulty might be restraining myself from picking locks or knocking out enemies.'

'Only in an emergency, dear,' said Mrs Carter. 'Do let me know how you get on, and if you wish, I would be happy to deliver further instruction.'

'Further instruction?' squeaked Maisie.

Mrs Carter laughed. 'You didn't think that was it, did you, Miss Frobisher? That was just the beginning.'

'It's, um, a kind offer,' said Maisie. 'But why me? I

mean, Inspector Hamilton —'

'I'm not particularly interested in Inspector Hamilton,' said Mrs Carter, 'except insofar as he relates to you. You could be very useful to me, Miss Maisie Frobisher.' She gave Maisie an appraising glance and rang the bell. 'Show Miss Frobisher out please, Avik,' she said. 'She has had enough for one day.'

'Maisie…?'

Maisie came to, and found Edward looking at her enquiringly. 'Did you hear what I said?'

'I'm so sorry,' said Maisie. 'I, um, something distracted me. Do repeat what you said, and I promise to listen this time.'

Edward blushed. 'I was — I was just saying that I hoped you could forgive my behaviour in Bombay, when I refused your invitation.'

'Did you?' said Maisie vaguely. 'I had forgotten.'

'Oh good!' cried Edward, smiling. 'There were so many rumours about you that I didn't know what to think, and I suppose… I suppose I got confused.' His smile became rather bashful. 'But I did — I mean I do — like you very much.'

Maisie smiled. 'I like you too, Edward.'

The waiter came, and she ordered her meal. 'I'll have the same,' said Edward. He put the menu aside with a sigh of relief, and sipped his glass of beer.

'Was that what you wanted to speak to me about?' asked Maisie.

Edward put down his glass. 'Partly.' He leaned forward. 'I also wanted to ask you if there had been any further developments about —' He leaned even closer. '*The murder*,' he whispered.

'It's an odd thing to say, but I'm glad you've mentioned it,' said Maisie. 'You see, we need to be very careful on Friday. Mr De Souza may be — connected — and he may not be all he seems.'

'Mr De Souza?' Edward said in his normal voice. 'Sorry,' he said, in response to Maisie's horrified shush. 'But he didn't seem the murdering type. A bit shady, perhaps.'

'So there is a murdering type?' Maisie couldn't help smiling. 'You must tell Inspector Hamilton.'

'Oh, Inspector Hamilton.' Edward Mandeville's tone made his opinion of that individual clear. Then he looked contrite. 'I hope he isn't a friend of yours, it's just that having worked with a man, one sees a different side of him. Nothing terrible, of course,' he said hastily.

'Perhaps we should leave Inspector Hamilton out of this,' said Maisie, though secretly she was pleased that someone else held her currently rather low opinion of Fraser. 'I must share some information with you. It comes from a reliable source.' Edward reached into his pocket for a notebook. 'No, you can't write it down. It is easy to remember. *The flamingo flies high.* It is a code phrase, and if our host says anything about birds, I intend to use it as a response.'

'But what does that have to do with — you know what?' asked Edward.

'It may help us to establish confidence,' said Maisie, racking her brains for a way to explain things to her companion. 'Like a password to a secret society.'

'Oh yes!' Edward's eyes shone. 'What else do I need to know?'

'There isn't much,' said Maisie. 'The main thing is to be your usual gentlemanly self, and if I signal that I want you to leave me alone for a while, you must do so.'

'But aren't I meant to be escorting you?' said Edward. 'I don't like the idea of leaving you on your own, especially if this man might be dangerous —'

'I won't be on my own,' said Maisie. 'You can stay within sight of me. But Mr De Souza may wish to tell me something privately. He indicated as much in his note to me. If I cannot give him that opportunity, the invitation is wasted.'

'I see.' Edward Mandeville regarded her speculatively. 'And I begin to see why you were so talked about in Bombay. Were you doing secret things there, too?'

Their starters arrived, and Maisie began hers to give her time to reply. 'It is nowhere near as exciting as you probably think,' she admitted finally. 'But I was involved in something, yes.'

'I thought so!' exclaimed Edward. 'I wonder what old Howarth would make of that, if he knew. He always liked you —' A sudden change came over his face. 'Where is Howarth? Is he really surveying, or is he mixed up in this too?'

Maisie chewed her food for some time. 'I don't know,' she said. 'I did see Mr Howarth on the train, but not since the day we arrived in Calcutta.'

'Oh.' Edward looked indescribably knowing. 'Then you

need say no more, Maisie.' He attacked his own dish. 'I say, this is rather good.'

He was as good as his word for the rest of the meal, keeping the conversation to light topics such as the latest novels, and the least venomous Bombay gossip. During dessert, he told her that he had checked the journey time, informed her at what time he would call for her, and assured her that he would wear a dinner jacket, in accordance with the dress code. They chatted in the carriage until they pulled up at Maisie's hotel. 'Till Friday, Maisie,' he said, taking her hand. He kissed it very gently, and held it in his for a moment. 'Though I wish I could have you all to myself again.' He smiled, rather sadly, and got out of the carriage to help her down.

Maisie bade him goodnight and went into the hotel, feeling dazed. *It is only the exercise*, she told herself. *But how nice to have an uncomplicated evening.* There had been no glowering, no resentment, no sniping. Apart from his opinion of Fraser — but she could hardly comment on that. *It is a refreshing change*, she thought, as Ruth helped her out of her dress and took down her hair. 'Did you have a nice evening, Miss Maisie?' she asked.

'Yes, I did,' said Maisie, looking at herself in the mirror. Lately, when returning from an encounter with Fraser, she had caught sight of herself frowning, but now she was serene. *And a change is as good as a rest.*

CHAPTER 15

'Is this what you were expecting?' Edward Mandeville asked in a low voice, as the carriage pulled up.

'I'm not sure what I was expecting,' said Maisie, 'but it wasn't this.' She eyed the bungalow, which showed lights in every window. People were spilling onto the front lawn, and she heard the thump of drums and the whine of instruments she couldn't identify. 'We don't have to stay long.'

Edward helped her out of the carriage, and tucked her arm firmly through his. 'Hold on tight, Maisie,' he said. Maisie's eyes widened. For the first time since her arrival in India, the majority of faces before her were not white. She felt rude for looking, and then realised everyone was looking at her. 'Let's go in,' she said, and everyone politely moved aside to let them through.

'Miss Frobisher! You came!' Mr De Souza appeared in

the entrance to the bungalow, framed in light. He wore a dinner jacket, well-cut but with slightly unusual lapels. 'And Mr Mandeville too,' he added. 'Come in, come in, and I shall find refreshment for you. Do you like the music?'

'It's charming,' Maisie said, raising her voice over it.

'Delightful,' added Edward. 'Very — different.'

'It is perhaps a different style from what you are used to,' said Anton De Souza. 'As you see, we have diverse company tonight, and therefore I must find music to suit them all.' He smiled. 'Later we shall have some good old English country dances.'

He led them into the parlour, whose furniture was mostly pushed back against the walls. Mr De Souza clicked his fingers, and a waiter appeared. 'Would sir and madam like a drink please,' he asked, all in one go.

'Lemonade, please, if you have it,' said Maisie. She would have preferred a glass of wine, but her head was spinning already.

'A glass of beer, please,' said Edward.

The servant bobbed and hastened away, and within a minute Maisie found a tall cold glass being pressed into her hand. 'Thank you,' she said, but the servant had already gone.

'It is a lovely night for a gathering,' said Mr De Souza. 'Very clear, and once the stars are out it will make for a pretty show. Would you like someone to take your shawl?'

'I shall keep it on,' said Maisie. 'I may need it if we go outside.'

'Do you get much wildlife around here, De Souza?'

asked Edward, and Maisie shot him a warning glance.

Mr De Souza laughed. 'You don't have to worry about that, Mr Mandeville. I can assure you that a tiger is most unlikely to appear in my garden. You may wish to watch out for snakes, but I have rarely encountered a venomous one.'

'Good heavens,' said Maisie. 'I hadn't thought of that.'

'Ah, that shows how new you are, Miss Frobisher,' said Mr De Souza. 'Most young ladies are excessively worried about being eaten by a tiger. The gentlemen, not so much,' he added, with a considering look at Edward Mandeville. 'They are usually more interested in shooting them.'

'What a waste of a tiger,' said Edward, his nose wrinkling. 'I would much rather shoot for the pot than for pleasure. A brace of partridge or a black buck, for instance, will be good spoils when I am surveying my district, as I shall be soon.'

'So long as you don't shoot any flamingos,' said Maisie, hastily. 'Such lovely birds. And they fly so high. The flamingos.'

Edward looked startled. 'Yes, I suppose they do,' he said. 'When they migrate, in particular.'

Mr De Souza seemed nonplussed. 'So you are a Civil Service man, Mr Mandeville?' he asked, as if trying to get the conversation back on a normal footing.

'Oh yes,' said Edward, with quiet pride. 'Almost six months now. I am usually in Bombay, but at present I have business in Calcutta.'

'I see,' said Mr De Souza. 'Do excuse me, more guests have arrived.' He bowed to them both, and strolled away.

Maisie shot an exasperated glance at Edward. 'What did you do that for?'

'I thought I'd bring up the topic of wildlife and see what happened,' Edward replied. 'I wasn't expecting you to dive in with a load of flamingos.'

'When you brought it up I thought I'd better,' Maisie retorted. 'After all, it isn't as if I could casually reintroduce the topic later in the evening.'

They glared at each other, then burst out laughing. 'At least it's done,' said Edward. 'Although I don't think he had a clue what we were talking about.'

'No,' said Maisie, taking a draught of her lemonade. 'Maybe my source was mistaken. I did try to get it as close to the right phrase as I could.'

'Oh, you did.' Edward drained his glass and clicked his fingers, but no waiter appeared. He tried again, with the same result. 'Clearly I don't have the magic touch,' he said ruefully. 'Shall I go and see what I can scare up?'

Maisie drained what was left in her glass. 'Yes please,' she said. 'Perhaps it will be cooler outside.'

'And quieter,' said Edward, taking her glass. 'Stay here, and when I have our drinks we can go out.'

Maisie eyed the small knots of people in the room, none of whom seemed disposed to welcome her to their conversation. Instead she wandered to the window and gazed out. She imagined the crickets chirping and playing their music, although that would probably be drowned by the artificial music and the chatter of Mr De Souza's guests. She wished she were outside; not in Mr De Souza's garden, amongst a crowd of people, but alone in a cool, quiet, fragrant place. She put her hand over her mouth to stifle a yawn. *Things have been so odd lately*, she thought. *And Fraser has been so . . . so hostile. Though perhaps if this is a red herring, and Leopard has nothing to do with Mr Ainsley's murder, things will return to normal. Whatever that is.* She leaned on the windowsill, her chin on her hands, and contemplated the scene.

'Why, Maisie, you're half-asleep!' cried Edward. 'I'm sorry I took so long. I found a waiter quite quickly, but he took an age to bring the drinks, and then I couldn't remember which way I came. The rooms look very similar, you see. Anyway, here is your lemonade.'

'Thank you,' said Maisie, smiling. 'And you haven't been long, only a few minutes. Come on, let's go outside.'

As they stepped onto the lawn Maisie realised the music had stopped. Then she heard stringed instruments tuning up, and a few seconds later they launched into a reel.

'Come on, everyone!' called Mr De Souza, hurrying to the centre of the lawn. 'Take your partners and form a line!' And so Maisie found herself dancing a Scots reel with Edward Mandeville, on the front lawn of a bungalow, beneath a Calcutta sky.

The band allowed them perhaps half a minute's breathing space between songs, and at the end of twenty minutes Maisie was gasping for breath. 'I shall sit out the next, if you don't mind,' she said, dropping Edward's hand and stepping out of the line.

'Oh, but it's capital fun!' Edward reached for her hand again. 'Please, Maisie?'

Maisie shook her head. 'I need a rest. I think the heat is getting to me.'

'Very well,' said Edward, though he looked a little disappointed. 'I'll take you inside. Unless you'd prefer a deckchair?' He glanced towards the rows of canvas chairs arranged at the side of the lawn, in which reposed several of the older guests.

'I shall try and find a lavatory,' said Maisie. 'If I splash my face with cold water that will help.'

'While you do that, I shall find myself another drink,' said Edward. 'Thirsty work, this.' He took Maisie's arm and led her into the hall, then hailed a servant for her, and strode off in search of refreshment.

Once Maisie had explained what she wanted, the servant crossed the hall and opened a little door. 'Running water, and fresh towels, ma'am.'

'Thank you so much,' said Maisie. She ran the tap for a few seconds until the water was as cold as it was going to get, and washed her face and hands. She wished she could have found a cold spring. Nevertheless, it was refreshing after her exertions; even listening to the water calmed her.

A few minutes later, Maisie emerged from the bathroom. *Where should I go now? Will Edward have found me a drink, too?* Perhaps he was still wandering in search of one. She was still smiling at that thought when Mr De Souza came out of a room at the back of the hall. He started when he saw her, but recovered himself quickly. 'Miss Frobisher, we meet again! Are you enjoying the dancing?'

'Oh yes, indeed,' said Maisie.

'In that case,' Mr De Souza said, shyly, 'may I have this dance?'

Maisie allowed her smile to broaden. 'Of course.'

Luckily the dance they joined was a couples-down-the-middle affair, which meant that Maisie and her partner spent much of the time standing still and clapping the others. When it was their turn to go down the middle, Mr De Souza proved nimble and light on his feet; though of course no one could compare with Fraser. And while Edward Mandeville was a perfectly adequate dancer — he galloped rather gallantly with a red-faced matron — he didn't come close. *It's a shame he isn't a better dancer*, she thought, then scolded herself severely.

They were called in for the buffet, which was a jumble of sandwiches and canapés and samosas and bhajis, with jugs of beer, punch, and lassi, and the gathering at last fell silent as everyone munched determinedly.

'What an evening,' said Maisie, under cover of her egg sandwich.

'I thought it was fun,' said Edward. 'You wouldn't get this in London.'

Maisie laughed. 'No, I don't suppose you would.'

'Did you enjoy yourself?' he asked later, in the carriage.

Maisie considered. 'We didn't get what we hoped for, but it was a nice evening.'

'I meant . . . with me,' he said quietly.

'Oh, Edward… I had a very nice time with you, but I must admit that I was focused on my task.' His expression was hard to read in the darkness. 'I apologise if I gave any sort of wrong impression.'

'Oh no, no, it isn't that. It's more... Well, I am rather awkward, and — I hope I didn't get in the way.'

Maisie could have laughed in her relief. 'Don't be silly,' she said, and tapped him with her fan. 'You helped me. Remember, with the flamingos?'

He laughed. 'How could I forget the flamingos? And I did leave you alone a couple of times, in case Mr De Souza wanted to talk to you.'

'There, you see, I didn't even realise,' said Maisie. 'That was very thoughtful of you.'

They subsided into silence, and Maisie yawned again. 'Here we are,' she said, as they reached her hotel.

'Indeed,' said Edward. He took her hand, but did not kiss it as he had the last time. 'Sleep well, Miss Frobisher, and thank you for a lovely evening.' He kept his eyes lowered as he handed her out, and gave her an odd, reserved look as he raised a hand in farewell.

Maisie dragged herself to her room with an effort, and rang for Ruth. 'I'm exhausted,' she said. 'Don't expect me to do a thing.'

Ruth raised her eyebrows. 'I won't, Miss Frobisher.' She eased Maisie's feet out of their shoes. 'A good evening, then?'

'An interesting evening,' replied Maisie. She closed her eyes and mused as Ruth bustled around. A strange evening, a disappointing evening, and a marvellous evening, all in one. But it had not gone as she had wanted. 'Never mind,' she said, 'there's always tomorrow,' and opened her eyes to see Ruth regarding her with utter bemusement.

CHAPTER 16

Maisie was woken by a gentle tapping at the door, which increased gradually in volume. *What time is it?* Early, unquestionably, but it was light outside. 'Yes?' she called.

'I have a telegram for you, Miss Frobisher.' A pause. 'Shall I put it under the door?'

Maisie yawned. 'What a good idea.' She got out of bed, padded to the door, and watched the yellow envelope come into view. 'Thank you,' she said, and ripped it open.

Sender: F Hamilton, Government House.
Please send word you are safe by return STOP F

'Is there an answer, madam?'

'Yes,' said Maisie, 'I shall write one now.' She pulled on a bed jacket, then sat at her desk with hotel notepaper and a pencil. After a moment's consideration, she wrote:

Yes I am safe and shall report GH this morning STOP M. She wrapped her jacket around her and delivered the note to the attendant, who was looking anywhere but at her. 'Could you bring tea, please?'

'Of course, madam,' he gabbled, and was gone before Maisie had closed the door.

Maisie arrived at Government House at ten o'clock and was shown into the waiting room, where Edward Mandeville was already seated. 'You got my wire, then?' she said.

'Oh yes,' said Edward. 'Thank you for including me.'

'Well, I could hardly not,' said Maisie, 'especially as you did half the work.'

'But it is nice to be acknowledged.' He beamed at her, and Maisie noted that he was very neat and immaculately dressed. *He is desperate to make a good impression*, she thought, and felt sad for him.

The servant reappeared. 'The viceroy will see you now.'

'So you came out unscathed,' were the viceroy's first words when they entered the study. His desk was clear, and he was in the act of filling his pipe. 'How did it go off?'

'We used the code phrase, Your Excellency, but De Souza showed no sign of recognition.' Edward Mandeville's voice was unexpectedly brisk, that of a man delivering bad news which can't be helped.

'No recognition, hey?' The viceroy's eyes narrowed. 'Could he have been faking it?'

'I don't think so,' said Maisie. 'We worked it into the conversation as best we could, but he just looked nonplussed and changed the subject. Later in the evening I was alone and Mr De Souza spoke to me, but he mentioned nothing of importance.'

'I see,' said the viceroy. 'Did you notice anything while you were there? Who were the other guests?'

'I recognised nobody,' said Maisie. 'It was a mixed company.'

'Some faces seemed familiar,' said Edward. 'I thought I recognised Miah, the editor of the *Messenger*, and at least two prominent Indian businessmen.'

'I see,' said the viceroy. 'Did De Souza talk with anyone in particular?'

'Not to my knowledge, Your Excellency,' said Edward. 'It was a noisy party, with music and dancing. As far as I could tell, Mr De Souza was focused on being a good host.'

'And that is a job which takes up an undue amount of time, as I know,' remarked the viceroy. 'Well done, both of you, I'm sure you did your best.' He looked at Edward Mandeville appraisingly. 'You seem a useful young man.'

Edward turned visibly pinker. 'Thank you very much, Your Excellency.'

'He was,' Maisie put in. 'I couldn't have delivered the code word without him.'

'Very good,' said the viceroy. 'I like to have useful people around me, so if you plan on staying for a while, there is plenty of accommodation here. Have a word with a servant on the way out, why don't you.' He mused for a moment. 'Shame about that code word, though. Perhaps Miss Jeroboam made a mistake.'

Maisie froze, but it was too late. 'Did you say Miss

Jeroboam?' Edward asked, with an odd look on his face.

The viceroy met Maisie's accusing eyes, and shrugged. 'I did. I thought you knew.'

Edward Mandeville's eyes were like saucers. 'She's alive?'

'She is, and under my protection,' said the viceroy.

'Good heavens,' breathed Edward. 'It's a miracle!' He turned to Maisie, and his face changed. 'Why didn't you tell me?'

Maisie fiddled with the bag on her lap. 'Nobody is meant to know she is alive,' she said quietly.

'But you know how much I admire her,' Edward said simply. He turned back to the viceroy. 'May I visit her?'

'She isn't very well,' Maisie began, but at a look from the viceroy she fell silent.

'I don't see why not,' said Lord Strathcairn. 'She's probably bored, stuck in that room with only Miss Frobisher to cheer her up. Maybe you can jog her memory a bit more, eh.' He opened a box on his desk and took out a book of matches. 'Why don't you take him up, Miss Frobisher, and see what Miss Jeroboam makes of him.'

Maisie fought her feelings all the way to Miss Jeroboam's rooms. *Why am I so reluctant? It isn't as if Edward's any sort of threat.* 'You do realise that no one else must know of this,' she said. 'Of course I know, and the inspector, and Captain James, but apart from that —'

'I shall say nothing to anyone,' said Edward.

'And you must be prepared for Miss Jeroboam's state of health,' Maisie added. 'She tires easily, and she has a bad cough, and she is often low in spirits.' Edward nodded, and looked straight ahead of him as if facing an ordeal.

They reached the door. 'Wait here,' said Maisie, and knocked.

'Who goes there?' called Miss Jeroboam.

'It is I, Maisie.'

'You may pass.'

Edward smiled at Maisie encouragingly. She ignored him, went in, and closed the door behind her. 'Charlotte, I have a visitor with me, but you don't have to see him if you don't want to. The viceroy thought it might be a good idea,' she said, in response to Miss Jeroboam's raised eyebrows.

'Who is he?' asked Miss Jeroboam. 'I assume it isn't the inspector in disguise.'

'I'm sure you see enough of him already,' replied Maisie. 'No, this young man is rather a fan of yours.'

'Oh, *that* young man,' said Miss Jeroboam, with a significant look at Maisie.

Maisie rolled her eyes. 'Do you want to meet him or not?'

Miss Jeroboam considered. 'I assume it is safe to do so. And in that case, why not.' She folded her hands in her lap. 'Show in the young gentleman.'

Maisie admitted Edward, who gazed at Miss Jeroboam in utter reverence. 'Miss Jeroboam, it is an absolute honour to make your acquaintance.' He advanced to the chair, crouched beside it, and bowed his head as if expecting to receive a blessing.

Miss Jeroboam gave him her hand, and laughed.

'Charlotte, this is Edward Mandeville,' said Maisie. 'He

is a great admirer of your work.'

'Oh, I am,' said Edward. 'I have read everything of yours that I can lay hands on. My favourite is your adventures in Africa.'

'Which are tame compared to what actually happened,' said Miss Jeroboam. 'The publisher made me cut out heaps on the grounds that people would never believe it.'

'Really?' said Edward.

'Oh yes,' said Miss Jeroboam. 'Pull up a chair, and I shall tell you what I remember. Maisie, would you mind ringing for tea?'

A half hour passed, then an hour. Maisie watched Miss Jeroboam keenly for signs of fatigue; but she did not seem tired. Her cheeks were pink — not the unhealthy flush of fever or over-exertion — and her eyes bright. *Perhaps Edward is doing what the rest of us could not*, she thought guiltily. *Accepting her for what she is.*

The clock chimed the half hour. 'Good heavens, is that the time?' exclaimed Edward. 'I could stay and listen to your tales all day, Miss Jeroboam, but I am afraid I have a lunch appointment.' He turned to Maisie. 'If it were anyone else I would break it, but it is my father, whom I have not seen for several years. We are both so busy that we have only just managed to arrange a meeting!'

'Then you must go,' said Miss Jeroboam. 'You may always come and visit me another day.'

'I would love to,' said Edward, 'if that were convenient.'

'Let me check my diary,' said Miss Jeroboam, not moving. 'Oh yes, I am always free. I would be delighted to see you, Mr Mandeville.'

Edward Mandeville took his leave of Miss Jeroboam and Maisie. 'Thank you so much for bringing me, Maisie,' he said. 'I am afraid I shall be busy for the rest of the day, since I shall probably move my traps this afternoon, but I shall be in touch soon.' He bowed to them both, and withdrew, shutting the door quietly behind him.

Miss Jeroboam waited a decent interval before laughing. 'He is like a new puppy,' she said. 'Although I must admit I did find his attention flattering.'

'I could tell,' said Maisie. 'You look almost your old self.'

'And there was I thinking that I was above such trivial things as flattery,' said Miss Jeroboam. 'He is a good listener, that young man, and he did have knowledge of my expeditions.'

'I told you he was a fan,' said Maisie.

'Do you know, I am rather hungry,' said Miss Jeroboam. 'Would you stay and take an early lunch with me, Maisie?'

'I had better go and see the inspector,' said Maisie, not without a touch of regret. 'He will want to know how we got on last night.'

'Oh yes, how was that?' Miss Jeroboam smiled. 'I assume Leopard didn't kill you both.'

'Not this time,' said Maisie. 'In fact, he didn't seem to recognise the code phrase at all.'

'Then I suppose he isn't the man,' said Miss Jeroboam. 'Well, you go and see your Inspector Hamilton. If you wish to look in later, I shall still be here.'

Maisie was shown straight in to the inspector, who was standing at the window. His shoulders were rigid. 'Good morning, Maisie,' he said. 'Anything to report?'

'Only a complete lack of reaction,' said Maisie. 'Edward and I did our best, but in the end it was just a jolly party.'

'Damn,' said Fraser. 'I hoped you might find something to incriminate Leopard, and then we could wrap this case up.'

'I take it you have no news,' said Maisie.

'No progress. No new evidence, no startling recollections,' said Fraser. 'This case is as dead as a dodo.' He glanced at Maisie. 'You could have wired last night to let me know you were safe,' he said accusingly.

'I'm sorry,' said Maisie. 'It was so not-dangerous that I completely forgot.'

'Oh yes, you and Edward.' Fraser shot her a scornful look.

'Why are you so down on him?' cried Maisie. 'What has he done to you?'

'Nothing,' said Fraser, with a tight smile. 'I'd like to see him try.'

'Maybe you will get the chance soon,' said Maisie. 'I believe he is moving into Government House. Perhaps you could room together.'

'*What?*' said Fraser.

'Yes, the viceroy suggested it this morning. So maybe you should think that over,' retorted Maisie, and walked out.

On the way home Maisie reflected that perhaps she had

been a little more angry with Fraser than he deserved. But really, his prejudice against Edward was ridiculous. *He wouldn't hurt a fly*, she concluded. *Look how well he did with Miss Jeroboam. Perhaps he will help her remember something vital, and then we can finish this case.*

And then what? But Maisie didn't want to think about that. She pushed the little voice away, and watched Calcutta go past outside the carriage window.

CHAPTER 17

Maisie jolted awake. Someone was at the door; but it was not the usual deferential tapping. *What is wrong? Is the hotel on fire?*

'What is it?' she called.

'I have an urgent telegram for you.' It was the concierge's voice.

'Could you put it under the door, please?'

A pause. 'I'm afraid I can't. I was instructed to make sure that you have opened it.'

Maisie got up, put on her bed jacket, and padded to the door, fuming. *If this is another of Fraser's urgent wires —*

'Please hurry, Miss Frobisher!' As Maisie opened the door he thrust the telegram into her hand. 'You must read it now.'

Maisie opened the envelope, watching him.

Report to Government House immediately STOP Strathcairn.

She looked up at the concierge. 'I take it no answer is required. Could you arrange a carriage for me?'

The concierge nodded as if his head would come off and backed away two steps before fleeing.

Maisie closed the door, and considered. She could ring and ask for Ruth; but by the time Ruth came to her she could be half-dressed. 'Best not to worry her,' she murmured, and went to the wardrobe.

As Maisie got ready an occasional question came to her. *What has happened? Is Fraser involved? Has someone else been murdered?* But mostly she just felt numb. Her fingers fumbled with the hooks and buttons until she wished she had summoned Ruth after all. But finally she was dressed, and her hair up somehow. She inspected herself in the glass with resignation. *I doubt anyone will have time to look at me, anyway*, she thought, and left.

The concierge was practically buzzing with impatience when Maisie walked into the foyer. 'The carriage is waiting; shall I take you, ma'am?'

'I can manage,' said Maisie, walking past him.

The streets were still quiet, and Maisie's numbness intensified to dread. *Please let everyone be all right*, she thought, gripping the handle of her bag to keep her hands from shaking. *Especially Fraser.* Their spat yesterday was forgotten in the light of something which sounded far worse.

Captain James was waiting at the top of the steps, and Maisie's heart sank at the expression on his face. 'Straight in please, Miss Frobisher.'

'Is it very bad?'

Captain James stepped aside to let her in without answering. 'The viceroy's study, please. I would take you, but I must remain here.'

Maisie hastened along the corridors which had become so familiar, but now stared back at her as if they had never seen her before. She tapped on the study door. 'Yes,' barked the viceroy, in a tone she barely recognised. She gritted her teeth, opened the door, and peeped round it. 'Come in and sit down.' Edward Mandeville was already seated in front of the desk, and looked as if he were trying not to cry.

'What has happened, Your Excellency?'

For answer, Lord Strathcairn jabbed at a newspaper lying face up on the desk. 'That.'

BRITISH DECEPTION
FALSE GOVERNMENT PAPERS CIRCULATED
ATTEMPTS TO DUPE HONEST CITIZENS

An anonymous source has revealed exclusively to this newspaper that undercover Government agents are circulating forged documents in an attempt to deceive the public. As proof, our source has furnished this newspaper with an agreement between Whitehall and the government of India which has demonstrably been falsified.

We understand that several prominent Indian citizens

have been separately furnished with this information, and await their reaction.

Maisie glanced at the masthead of the paper. *The Clarion*, it proclaimed.

'The most popular newspaper among those of the Indian population who can read,' said the viceroy, and jabbed at it again. 'What the *hell* did you say to De Souza to make him do this?'

'Nothing!' cried Maisie.

'You must have done something,' snapped the viceroy. 'He's had that document ever since Howarth handed it to him, and only now has he made use of it. Think, damn it! And you'd better think fast, because I've sent Hamilton to bring De Souza in, and I want your version before I hear what he has to say.'

Maisie swallowed. 'I have already told you what happened when we went to Mr De Souza's house. We tried the code phrase and it had no effect, so we stayed for the rest of the party. I spent some time alone in case he wished to talk to me, but he did not.'

The viceroy banged his fist on the desk and glared at Maisie. 'You're no more use than he is,' he said, and the contempt in his voice was far worse than if he had shouted at her. 'If that's the best you can do, go and wait in the anteroom until you are sent for.'

Maisie and Edward rose, thanked the viceroy, and left. They did not speak again till they were seated in the familiar waiting room. There they could hear the front door opening, and raised not-British voices, followed by the quieter tones of Captain James insisting that the viceroy was not available.

'That sounds like the prominent Indian citizens,' murmured Edward, and every freckle on his face stood out against the white skin.

'Oh dear,' said Maisie. 'What can they do?'

'I don't know,' said Edward. 'The best we can hope for is that Hamilton finds proof, or De Souza admits it.'

They fell silent; what was the point of talking? Then a flurry of footsteps entered the hall, and a voice cried, 'I demand my rights! You can't do this!'

It was Anton De Souza's voice.

'This way, please.' The voice was not Fraser's, and Maisie looked at Edward with sudden dread.

'Hamilton has orders to search De Souza's house,' said Edward, his voice flat. 'The viceroy told him not to return until he found something.'

The footsteps and De Souza's angry voice died away, and they waited.

'How was your father?' asked Maisie, for the want of anything else to say.

Edward looked blank for a moment. 'Oh yes. He is well. We had a nice lunch.' He smiled briefly. 'I had almost forgotten, with all this.' They fell silent, and watched the second hand of the clock crawl round the dial.

A tap at the door made Maisie jump. 'Could you come to the viceroy's study, please, Miss Frobisher,' said the servant, his face blank.

Lord Strathcairn looked even angrier than he had at the first meeting. 'Sit, please,' he said curtly.

Maisie obeyed, not daring to glance to her right, where Mr De Souza sat flanked by two policemen.

'To put it in a nutshell, Miss Frobisher, Mr De Souza denies having anything to do with a certain document which has just been circulated about the Indian community and linked to a popular newspaper.' The viceroy paused. 'I would like you to provide your own account of events, please, from the point when you answered an advertisement in the *Bombay Telegraph*.'

In a halting voice, Maisie began, speaking of the strange advertisements, her journey to Calcutta, the meeting where Mr Howarth had taken the forged document from her, and her witnessing of the same document being handed to Mr De Souza. He breathed hard, but said nothing.

'How can you deny having anything to do with this, De Souza?' The viceroy leaned forward. 'You have been positively identified as being in possession of it.'

Anton De Souza shrugged. 'How do you know it is the same document? Miss Frobisher's own account states that I did not read it, but put it away. For all you know, it was a laundry list.' His voice was calm, measured, with the lilt that Maisie remembered from that very meeting. She looked across, and started when she met his eyes. 'Miss Frobisher, I am disappointed that when I met you at the viceroy's reception your interest in me was as false as this document apparently is. I would certainly not have invited you to my home if I had known that. However, it is not your fault that you were a pawn in the viceroy's game.' His glance flicked to the chessboard set up in a corner. 'Was that what all that chatter about flamingos was for? A silly code-word?' He laughed. 'You British, with your "intelligence" and your "great game". You have tried to manoeuvre me into a corner, Viceroy, but you will find that I too have allies on the board.'

Another tap at the door. 'What is it?' barked the viceroy.

'Inspector Hamilton has returned, Your Excellency.'

'Good, show him in.' The viceroy drummed his fingers on the leather-topped desk. 'Now we shall see.'

Fraser entered the room. 'Your Excellency, I had hoped to see you alone,' he said, glancing at the other occupants.

'Given what has happened this morning, there's no chance of that,' replied the viceroy. 'What have you found?'

Fraser said nothing.

'Out with it!' cried the viceroy.

Fraser looked straight ahead, his face expressionless. 'I have found nothing, Your Excellency. There were no incriminating documents at Mr De Souza's house.'

'Then search again,' said the viceroy. 'You must have missed something.'

Fraser shook his head. 'We have taken apart the desk, rolled back the carpets, and searched all the cupboards, as well as inside the cushions and the mattress. If there was ever anything incriminating there, it is not there now.'

'You searched my bungalow?' shouted Mr De Souza. 'You took apart my belongings, and destroyed my things?' He had a strange smile on his face. 'I should be thankful that you have not planted evidence. I shall make sure that everyone of my acquaintance knows of this shameful treatment.' He stood up. 'As you found nothing, you have no case against me.' The policemen looked at each other, then at the viceroy, but did not move. 'You think you may do what you like, *Your Excellency,* but you haven't heard the last of this!' The door slammed behind him.

The viceroy was silent, and Maisie's heart was a tight knot in her chest. Then he spoke, in a quiet, distinct voice. 'I was a fool to believe any of the rigmarole you presented me with. My instincts told me it was far-fetched, and I should have trusted them, instead of encouraging two children playing at spies.' He glared at Maisie. 'Miss Frobisher, I suppose I could expect nothing better from you, as someone who is not a member of the Service and has no understanding of what they are getting into.' Maisie winced; but the viceroy had already turned to Fraser.

'Inspector Hamilton, as a policeman of avowed seniority, I consider you responsible for this. In addition, despite having the considerable resources of Government House at your disposal, you have made no progress whatsoever in the Ainsley investigation.' He paused, and the next words rapped out as if he were pronouncing sentence. 'As far as I am concerned, Inspector, you are no longer in my service. I shall also write to Lord Montgomery and advise him to discharge you. In my opinion, the best thing for you to do is return to England, and there limit yourself to matters within your competence. Now go, and leave me to deal with the consequences of your actions.'

CHAPTER 18

Maisie had no memory of leaving the room, or of what she had said to the viceroy. She found herself half-walking, half-stumbling along the corridor, with Fraser's arm firmly through hers. 'What happens now?' she whispered.

'We go and pack,' said Fraser. His face was so rigid that it could have been chiselled from stone. 'I intend to leave by the first train possible, and I assume that you do too.'

'I — I hadn't thought,' said Maisie. Her brain felt numb, as an arm feels numb when you bump it hard against something.

Fraser halted suddenly and stared at her. 'You can't want to stay, after what the viceroy said?'

'It isn't that,' said Maisie. 'I never expected —'

'So you've learnt a lesson today, Maisie.' Fraser's voice was harsh. 'You're privileged as long as you're useful, and the moment that ends, you take the blame.' He resumed his walk, but more slowly. 'After that treatment, I won't stay a minute longer than I have to.' He looked down at Maisie. 'Do you need me to see you to the hotel?'

'I don't think I can bear it yet,' said Maisie. 'I don't think I'm ready to tell Ruth that we're going.' The idea of being scared of one's maid made her giggle, and she found she could not stop.

'I don't think you're ready to go anywhere,' said Fraser. 'Come to the office while I get things in order. You can sit quietly there, and no one will bother us.'

It seemed as good an idea as any, and presently Maisie was sitting at Fraser's desk watching him put papers into files, and files into drawers. 'Why was the case so hard?' she said suddenly.

'There was nothing to get hold of,' Fraser replied, closing the drawer sharply. 'No murder weapon to find, because it was already at the scene. The murderer should have been covered in blood, but wasn't. I doubt the murderer even knew that Ainsley would be there, since Mrs Carter got him in at the last minute. Someone should have seen something, but nobody did.' He stared blankly at the piece of paper in his hand. 'I wonder who will take over.'

Maisie shrugged. 'I imagine the viceroy would say that was none of our business.'

'Probably,' said Fraser. 'I've finished, more or less. Shall I find you a carriage? Would you like me to come with you?'

'I'm sure I can manage,' said Maisie. She got up, but the act of standing made her head swim. She sat back down and grabbed the desk for support. 'Oh!'

'Maisie, what is it?' Fraser was beside her in a moment, supporting her with an arm. 'You looked as if you were about to faint.'

'I thought I might.' Maisie's stomach growled, and she managed a weak smile. 'I haven't had breakfast. That must be what it is.'

Fraser made sure that she was sat squarely in the chair, then rang the bell. 'Tea and biscuits, please,' he told the servant.

'Fraser, no!' cried Maisie. 'What will the viceroy say?'

'What will he do, sack me?' There was no mirth in Fraser's laugh. 'I'm not having you fainting all over Calcutta.'

'I just don't understand,' said Maisie. 'It seemed to be going so well.' Then she frowned. Had it? She closed her eyes, and thought. It had begun well, with the reappearance of Miss Jeroboam, her recall of the code phrase, and Leopard's interest in her at the reception; but from that point things had gone decidedly wrong. 'At least we can see the Pyramids now,' she said, and burst into tears.

'Oh, Maisie…' Fraser put his arms round her, and held her close. 'At least you haven't been banned from the captain's table this time.' A tap sounded at the door. 'Could you put it on the table, please,' he called.

'It's worse!' sniffled Maisie. 'I've made India too hot to hold me!'

'I wouldn't be too sure of that,' said Mrs Carter's voice. 'Sorry about the slight delay, I sent the servant back for an extra cup.'

They sprang apart and goggled at her. 'What are you doing here?' said Maisie. 'I mean, good morning, but —'

'Avik brought me the *Clarion* this morning at breakfast, and it became apparent that I might be needed,' said Mrs Carter. 'I caught the viceroy as he was packing young Mandeville off to the *Clarion* offices to see what could be done. I doubt anything can be done, though, since the cat is not just out of the bag, but capering merrily around Calcutta.' She snorted. 'Leopard may be having his fun now, but he will get what's coming to him, never you fear. I shall see to that myself.' She raised an eyebrow. 'Shall I pour?'

Maisie accepted a strong cup of tea with plenty of sugar, and took a biscuit. 'So . . . is Mr Mandeville staying on?'

'Apparently,' said Mrs Carter. 'And I don't think you should pack your bags yet, either.'

'But the viceroy told us to go,' said Maisie.

'I'm sure he did,' said Mrs Carter. 'However, if he was in a similar mood to the one I happened upon him in, I don't think it will last. For one thing, I told him to calm down and behave like a rational being.'

'You didn't,' breathed Maisie.

'Oh, I did,' said Mrs Carter. 'That is what he must do, and he knows it. Clearly he was taking out his frustration with the Leopard matter on you.'

'But what shall we do?' asked Maisie. 'We can't just sit here and wait to be called back in.'

'And what if I won't work for the viceroy?' said Fraser.

'Is your pride so very important, compared with the

fate of a nation?' asked Mrs Carter.

Fraser looked at his feet, and said nothing.

'I thought not.' She drained her cup, and set it on the tray. 'Now, I suspect Mr Mandeville will uncover no trace of Leopard at the *Clarion*; after all, the man is not a fool. In that case, either Mr De Souza has covered his tracks impeccably — which is possible but unlikely — or someone else is the anonymous informant. I'll let you consider that.' She stood up. 'Miss Frobisher, you know where you can find me. Inspector, you are also welcome to call. For now, I shall let you get on.'

'Well,' said Fraser, once the door had closed. 'Now we have conflicting orders. And I am not sure whether it is better to disobey the viceroy, or Mrs Carter.'

Maisie shivered and put her cup of tea down hastily, for her hand was trembling.

'Have another biscuit,' said Fraser, passing the plate.

'It isn't that,' said Maisie. 'What if —' She fiddled with the clasp of her bag. 'What if the phrase Miss Jeroboam gave us wasn't a password, but a warning?'

'You mean she might have alerted Leopard that you were on his track?' Fraser pushed his hair off his forehead. 'That doesn't sound like her. Whatever her faults, Miss Jeroboam isn't the sort of person to stab you in the back.'

'I know,' said Maisie. 'It's an explanation that makes sense, but you're right.' She picked up her cup again, and sipped meditatively. 'I shall go and see her, and ask if I may read the recollections she wrote down. They might help.'

'It's worth a try,' said Fraser. 'While you do that, I'll

reread the statements from the reception. We've been torn in two directions for so long that I could easily have missed something.'

Maisie found Miss Jeroboam studying a newspaper, pen in hand. 'Good morning, Maisie,' she said, looking up with a smile. 'You're early.'

'That isn't the *Clarion*, is it?' asked Maisie.

'The *Clarion*?' Miss Jeroboam sounded puzzled. 'No, this is the *Messenger*. Mr Mandeville brought it for me. He said he thought my brain needed stimulation, and recommended the word-cross puzzle.' She rubbed her forehead. 'We did one together when he called, but I can barely make head or tail of this.'

Maisie peered over her shoulder, and read a couple of clues. 'Me neither,' she said. 'How is one supposed to solve that?'

'I know!' Miss Jeroboam laughed and laid down her pen. 'I assume that you came to see me for a reason, Maisie, as it is rather early for a social call.'

'Yes,' said Maisie. 'If you don't mind, could I read your recollections?'

'I can't see any reason why not,' said Miss Jeroboam, 'except for my personal pride. There is more crossing-out than writing, and what is there makes little sense.' She opened the drawer of the table and drew out a few sheets of paper. 'I have added a little more, and you're welcome to it all.'

'Thank you,' said Maisie, and settled to read. The task was not easy, since the narrative did not flow; it was a jumble of broken phrases and single words followed by question marks. But something else, something just out of reach, distracted Maisie. *What is it?* She closed her eyes and rubbed them with her fingertips.

'That's exactly how I feel about this puzzle,' said Miss Jeroboam.

Maisie stared at her, and blinked. 'Yes,' she said. 'I wonder if one needs to have the right sort of brain for word-cross puzzles, or whether there is a knack to it. Do you still have the one that you did with Mr Mandeville?'

'I think it is in the waste-paper basket,' said Miss Jeroboam, leaning down and picking it up. 'Yes, here.'

Maisie fished out the newspaper and opened it to the right page. The puzzle was neatly filled in, in a single hand, with no erasures. The hand was not Miss Jeroboam's.

1 across: *PARLIAMENT.*
Maisie looked for the clue. *A court of partial men (10).*
7 down: *ANEMONE. Name one flower (7).*
15 across: *REFEREES. Send on and look back (8).*

Maisie frowned. With the answers written in, the clues made sense, but —

What sort of mind can work this out so easily?
A quick, agile, devious mind…
Yet that's completely unlike the Edward Mandeville I know.

'Looking at this puzzle,' she said, gazing at the newspaper, 'I think it does require a particular type of brain. Would you mind if I took this away and studied it?'

'Not at all,' replied Miss Jeroboam. 'It is of no use to me.'

Maisie hardly dared breathe as she got herself out of the room. *It is only a word-cross puzzle*, she told herself. *A puzzle; a diversion; something to occupy one at breakfast, or perhaps on a train journey.* But even as she thought it, Maisie found she was gripping the paper tighter and tighter, till it threatened to tear, and she found herself running through the corridors of Government House, that great maze of bureaucracy. And the heart of that maze was Fraser's office.

CHAPTER 19

Fraser stared at her. 'That's ridiculous.'

'I know it's ridiculous,' said Maisie. 'But that doesn't mean it can't be true.' She dropped the newspaper on the desk. 'Look at this.'

Fraser looked. 'So Mandeville is good at puzzles,' he said, with a hint of a smile.

'He worked in the same office as Howarth. He was the last person who saw Ainsley alive, as far as anyone can make out. And when he came with me to Leopard's house, we were apart for a while. He said it was to give me time to speak to Leopard alone, but the same applies to him.'

'Theoretically, it makes sense,' said Fraser. 'But Mandeville is so *dim*.'

'Unless he isn't,' argued Maisie. 'He shouldn't be. He's been to university and he knows all sorts of classical languages.'

'All that proves is that he has a good memory,' replied Fraser.

'And the puzzles?'

'All right, and a facility for solving quizzes. Anyway, it makes no sense. Mandeville would go straight from university to Civil Service studies, and then out here. His father is a high-ranking civil servant, for heaven's sake!'

'I wonder if he did go to see him,' said Maisie. 'When we visited Miss Jeroboam the other day, he excused himself because he said he was lunching with his father.'

'There, you see?' Fraser began to smile; but then it vanished, and the colour drained from his face. 'Don't tell me Mandeville's father is mixed up in this. He has connections everywhere, and would know how to leak information for the greatest effect. That would be devastating.'

'Wait a minute,' said Maisie. 'Just now you thought I was being ridiculous.'

'And perhaps you still are,' said Fraser. 'But it's too serious a risk not to investigate.'

'Very well,' said Maisie. 'Where do we start?'

'As Mandeville is out, let's try his rooms,' said Fraser. 'Perhaps we can persuade someone to let us in.'

'Somehow I doubt it,' said Maisie. 'I have a better idea.' She opened her bag and fished out a packet of hairpins. 'Let's see if I can get these to work.'

***

'You're full of surprises, Maisie Frobisher,' murmured Fraser as the door swung open.

'Never mind that,' said Maisie. 'Inside, quick! We may

not have long.'

Edward Mandeville had travelled light, and his traps, as he called them, did not take up much room. Fraser opened the wardrobe and thrust his hand into the pockets of a tweed jacket. 'Try the chest of drawers, Maisie,' he said.

'If you don't mind, I'd rather leave that to you,' said Maisie. She went to the desk, on which was a letter case. Within were five or six letters, addressed, stamped, and sealed. 'That's odd,' she said, frowning. 'Isn't Government House mail franked?'

'Yes, it is,' said Fraser, coming to look. 'That's quite an extensive correspondence for someone who has only been here a few days.' He pointed to the address on the first letter. 'Who would Mandeville know in Bangalore?'

'It could be someone he knows from university,' said Maisie. 'Someone that he studied with before he came to India.'

'I doubt it,' said Fraser, moving his finger higher. 'Mrs…?' They exchanged glances. 'What I wouldn't give at this moment to rip these letters open and go through them!'

'We can't,' said Maisie. 'We can copy the names and addresses, and that's all.' Fraser pulled out a notebook, and she wandered to the shelf. On it were a Bible, a cheap paperback novel, and a copy of *Wisden Cricketer's Almanack*. Maisie leafed through the pages of the novel, but they told her nothing. The Bible, however, told a slightly different story; every so often, a verse had been underlined. Maisie read the verses, but could find no connection between them. 'Perhaps he just liked them,' she said aloud.

'Liked what?' asked Fraser, looking up from his notebook.

'He has underlined some verses in his Bible,' said Maisie, closing the book.

'Let me see.' Fraser began to page through the book from the beginning. 'One verse in each of the first three books. Make a note of the numbers, Maisie. They may be the key to a cypher. I have two more addresses to copy, then I'll look at the almanac.'

They worked quickly, but as Maisie scribbled on a torn-out page from Fraser's notebook she worried that they would be discovered. 'We should go,' she said. 'If he finds us here —'

'The game is probably up,' said Fraser. 'The almanac seems clean, anyway.' He put away his notebook and carefully lifted the mattress on the neatly-made bed. 'Nothing there. But you're right, Maisie. I think we have something. Why on earth would Mandeville be sending letters all over India?' He remade the bed quickly. 'Let's go. And if you can re-lock the door with one of your hairpins, that would be marvellous.'

***

'What now?' asked Maisie, once they were distant enough from Edward Mandeville's room to appear innocent.

'This may sound odd,' said Fraser, 'but I would like to go and see Howarth. Not because I think he has been shielding Mandeville — he was so generous with his information that he would have given away his own grandmother if he had thought it would help. Just to see what he thought of him.'

'You said he was dim,' said Maisie.

'I was rather forthright in my opinion,' said Fraser. 'I don't think I meant dim, exactly. More . . . content to be mediocre. I'm not even sure what he did all day in Bombay.'

'Do you think we'll be able to see Mr Howarth?' asked Maisie.

'I don't see why not,' Fraser replied. 'I doubt the viceroy has had a chance to warn the police station about me yet.'

***

'More questions?' The policeman scratched his head. 'Very well, Inspector. I'll go and see what state he is in.' He retrieved a large ring of keys from the drawer, and wandered off, whistling.

A few minutes later he returned. 'The gentleman will see you now, Inspector.' He gawped at Maisie. 'Oh no, I don't think a police-station cell is a fit place for a young lady.'

'Then bring him to another room,' said Fraser, 'and give him a cup of tea.'

The policeman regarded him, sucking his teeth. 'All right,' he said, at last. 'Whatever sir wants.'

Mr Howarth was not quite a shadow of his former self, but thinner, less solid, and looking perhaps five years older. He also appeared extremely tired. 'Inspector Hamilton,' he said, rising as the policeman showed them into the room. 'To what do I owe the pleasure?' He spoke slowly, seeming to roll the words around his mouth. Maisie suspected he had not spoken to anyone for some time.

'If you wouldn't mind waiting outside the door,' Fraser said to the policeman, who huffed and obeyed. 'Mr Howarth, if anyone asks, you haven't seen me or Miss Frobisher. I would like to ask you a couple of questions concerning one of your staff, Edward Mandeville.'

'Oh no, he had nothing to do with it —'

'That isn't what I mean,' said Fraser. He leaned forward. 'The thing is, Mandeville is up for a sort of promotion, and despite your current status, you were his supervisor.'

'I was, wasn't I?' said Mr Howarth, as if that had been years ago. He thought for a moment. 'Mandeville, a promotion?'

'I must confess that I was surprised,' said Fraser.

'Yes,' said Mr Howarth. 'I don't want to speak out of turn, but I was disappointed in that young man. He came to us with such an excellent reputation. A first-class degree at Oxford, and classical languages, and first place in several of the Civil Service examinations. Not to mention his family…'

'Do you mean that he was not as clever as you thought?' asked Maisie.

'Not so much that,' said Mr Howarth, 'but completely without motivation or ambition. I tried to interest him in the workings of the Service, and the various career paths open to a promising young griffin such as himself, but he seemed content with the simplest of tasks; the sorts of things a clerk could do. After a month or two I am afraid I simply gave him up as a bad job, and entrusted him with tasks which didn't matter too much if he got them wrong. Compiling statistics, filing reports, even carrying messages.' He smiled. 'It was rather soothing to have someone like that working for me; someone who I knew would not try to overreach me, or seek preferments over my head. Why, you could have left him alone with a file of state secrets and I doubt he would have bothered to open it, such was his lack of curiosity.'

'How odd,' said Fraser. 'Was he enthusiastic about anything?'

'Oh, any kind of sport,' said Mr Howarth. 'Then again, most of the youngsters are. What else is there to do? I remember him being keen to get up a rugby team, till I explained we would have no one to play against. That was his schooling coming out.'

'Oh yes, didn't he go to Rugby?' asked Fraser.

'He did,' said Mr Howarth. 'He boasted about it rather. That, and Oxford. I found it distasteful.'

'I'm inclined to agree with you,' said Fraser. 'Thank you, Mr Howarth, this has been most illuminating. It will help me considerably in my recommendation.'

'You won't tell Mandeville that I have spoken ill of him, will you?' asked Mr Howarth.

'Your secret is safe with me,' said Fraser. 'Thank you for your time.' And Mr Howarth performed a jerky little bow as they took their leave.

Maisie half-ran to keep up with Fraser as he strode through the station. 'What is it?'

'A hunch which I must check.' He hailed a rickshaw.

'Back to Government House.'

A servant admitted them, looking full of news. 'Mr Mandeville has asked me to inform you that he wishes to see you as soon as possible,' he said.

'Very well,' said Fraser. 'I must just attend to one thing first. Do excuse me.' He made for the stairs before the servant had a chance to say any more.

'He'd better not have got to them yet,' he said, taking the stairs two at a time. They reached the cramped little room they had used as an office at the beginning of their residency, and he removed the lid of the box marked *Saunders*. 'Here.' He passed Maisie a handful of files.

'What am I looking for?'

'Saunders's schooling.' Fraser extracted more papers and dropped them on the desk, then stared into the box. 'I don't believe it.' He lifted out a photo of a team in striped jerseys and short trousers. In the centre a boy held a trophy, and his right foot rested on a rugby ball. *First Eleven, Rugby School, May 1883*. He turned the photograph over. 'There he is.' He scrutinised the front briefly, then handed the photograph to Maisie. 'Second row, third from the right. F Saunders.'

Maisie stared at the boy in the picture. He was still a boy, just about, but tall, and slender for a rugby player. 'Perhaps he outgrew his strength,' she said softly. 'I wonder what made him do it?'

'So do I,' said Fraser. 'But that's for another time. We must get to the viceroy and make him listen, before more damage is done.' He picked up the photograph and threw open the door.

'And what if he doesn't believe us?' said Maisie, as they hastened down the corridor.

'He has to believe us,' said Fraser. 'Given what we've discovered today, Mandeville, that dim, snobbish fool, may be the most dangerous man I have ever set eyes on.'

CHAPTER 20

'He's late,' said Maisie.

'He is,' said Fraser. 'And while the viceroy's invitation was distinctly humble, I'm not sure it's a good idea to keep him waiting.'

As if on cue, a distant bell rang. Maisie's heart leapt, and she clutched at Fraser's arm.

'Calm down!' said Fraser, laughing. 'He can probably hear your heartbeat from outside the door.'

Maisie took several deep breaths, gulping for air like a stranded fish.

Fraser studied her. 'I'm not sure that will help,' he whispered. 'But if it makes you feel better, do continue.'

The door opened, and they heard Captain James's voice. 'If you would come this way, Mr De Souza. As we are a small party, we shall dine in the red room tonight.'

'A small party,' murmured Leopard's voice. 'Very

good.' His tone had the suggestion of a purr. 'I suppose the viceroy wishes to keep his apology private.'

'Oh, it is not that,' said Captain James. 'I'm sure any apology the viceroy makes will be full, frank and public. However, I believe he desires to talk to you about working more closely together, and such discussions are, naturally, not for everyone's ears.'

'That was smooth,' said Maisie, in admiration.

'James earns his money,' Fraser replied.

The footsteps drew closer, until it seemed that the pair would enter their room. Fraser winced as Maisie gripped his arm; but the door which opened was not theirs.

'Mr De Souza,' said the viceroy genially. 'Thank you for accepting my invitation. I was somewhat concerned that you might think better of it.'

'I hope I'm a bigger man than that,' said Mr De Souza. 'I was, of course, exceedingly angry to be dragged before you, and even more so when I discovered that you had ransacked my house. But I understand why you did it, and I'm prepared to let bygones be bygones.' He paused. 'However, I am surprised that Mr Mandeville is joining us.'

'Ah,' the viceroy replied. 'Mr Mandeville's part in your, um, apprehension, while regrettable, has been relatively minor, and therefore I am giving him a second chance. He is young enough to learn not to meddle in things which do not concern him.'

'Thank you, Your Excellency,' murmured Edward Mandeville.

'No need to thank me,' said the viceroy. 'However, Mr

De Souza, you may be confident that Inspector Hamilton and Miss Frobisher have been dealt with as they deserve.'

Everyone fell quiet for a moment, and Maisie heard the servants' light footsteps, and the trickle of wine into glasses. 'May I propose a toast,' said the viceroy. 'To working in partnership!'

'To working in partnership,' echoed the rest of the party.

'Before the first course arrives,' said the viceroy, 'I wish to apologise. You were quite right, Mr De Souza. I ought never to have supposed that it was you who leaked a stolen document to the papers, and exposed it as a forgery. For one thing, how would you have known it was a forgery?'

'Precisely,' said Mr De Souza.

'And why would a merchant get involved in providing information to the newspapers for free?' The viceroy's tone was dangerously smooth. 'As a good businessman, you would be much more inclined to sell it.'

'I'm not sure I understand what you mean,' said Mr De Souza.

'Don't worry, I shall explain myself,' said the viceroy. 'But first I shall also state that I do not believe you to be the murderer of Thomas Ainsley. What point would there be to that? After all, you would hardly engage in such activity under my nose. That isn't your style.'

Mr De Souza began to mutter, but the viceroy held up a hand. 'Back to the matter in hand. I know you received the forged document from Mr Howarth. However, my belief is that you were merely a link in a long chain of operatives, within which you would only know as much about the next link as you needed to. Your job was merely to keep the document until it was required, then pass it on.'

'How dare you,' said Mr De Souza. 'You invite me here under false pretences, and make unsupported accusations —'

'Not unsupported,' said the viceroy. He stood, and rang the bell. 'Don't even think about moving, Mr De Souza.'

'Here we go,' murmured Fraser, and opened the connecting door.

It was hard to tell whether Leopard or Edward Mandeville looked the more surprised, but De Souza was the first to find his voice. 'You said —'

'I said they had been dealt with,' replied the viceroy. 'I didn't say how. At first, in my anger, I blamed them. Luckily for me, both Miss Frobisher and Inspector Hamilton had the grace and determination to keep searching for proof to back up their case. Presently, they found it.'

'They can't have!' cried Mr De Souza. 'There's nothing to find!'

'Not against you,' said the viceroy. 'Against Mr Mandeville.'

Edward Mandeville gasped. 'I say, what on earth do you mean?' he stammered.

He began to get up, but Captain James casually drew a gun and covered him with it. 'I suggest you stay seated, Mandeville.'

'But what am I supposed to have done?' Mandeville cried, in the tone of a child who has been scolded and can't understand why.

'We'll begin with our visit to Mr De Souza's house,' said Maisie. 'You assisted me in a bungling way with the code phrase, which would probably alert Mr De Souza — or should I say Leopard? — to the fact that something was wrong. Mr De Souza excused himself promptly, and had no further meaningful engagement with me that evening. However, I was alone for part of the evening, and therefore, so were you. That is when I believe that identification was made, and the forged document passed over. Mr De Souza would not know enough about the document to recognise it as a forgery, but you would.'

'But it doesn't make any sense,' said Edward Mandeville. 'Why would I do something like that? Why would I want to?'

'Let's move on to the next day,' said Maisie. 'The viceroy accidentally let slip that Miss Jeroboam was not only still alive, but residing in Government House. You were keen to see her, and I suspect the reason was not your admiration for her discoveries, but desperation to know what she might have revealed.'

'I do admire Miss Jeroboam's discoveries!' exclaimed Edward Mandeville, looking hurt.

'Perhaps you do,' Maisie replied. 'However, you had another important task that day; to spread news of that document. Therefore you excused yourself to have lunch with your father. That was when you tipped off the *Clarion*, and posted your letters to as many prominent Indian people as you could think of. But you had not forgotten your new friend. You visited her again, bringing her puzzles to strengthen her brain and improve her memory. If you befriended Miss Jeroboam, there was a chance that you could either know what she had shared, or lead her recollections down false paths.'

'But I *did* lunch with my father,' insisted Edward Mandeville. 'And when would I have found time to write these letters?'

'You are a prolific letter-writer, Mandeville,' said Fraser. 'When we visited your room the other day we found several in your letter case, addressed to men and women all over India.'

'You were in my room?' Mandeville cried. 'Who let you in?' He turned to the viceroy. 'This is an outrage.'

'I am afraid I picked the lock,' said Maisie. 'We were tempted to take your letters and look inside, but we decided that would be going too far.'

'I should think so,' he replied, with an air of ruffled self-righteousness.

'However,' Maisie continued, 'when we laid the evidence before the viceroy, he agreed it would be perfectly acceptable for Inspector Hamilton to intercept your letters at the post office, as a matter of national security.'

'And working with the numbers which I found in your Bible, in the guise of underlined verses,' said Fraser, 'I found the same message in every letter. *Ready part three.*'

Mandeville swallowed. 'That must be a coincidence,' he said.

'I don't think so,' replied Fraser.

'All right. The letters were a silly joke, no more.'

Edward Mandeville ran a finger round the inside of his collar. 'A running joke between me and some old friends. It means nothing.'

'Oh, that's a relief,' said the viceroy. 'In that case we may proceed to the murder.'

'What murder?' said Mandeville; but he said it quietly, and Maisie saw his eyes dart around the room, seeking a way out. Under cover of the table, she opened her bag.

'Thomas Ainsley was a merchant, like yourself, Mr De Souza,' said Fraser. 'However, he was also an agent working for the viceroy. That fact was known to very few people, since he was extremely good at his job. However, he was murdered at the viceroy's reception. Why? Everyone who knew he would be there was trustworthy, and there was no reason to suppose his identity had been discovered.'

'That is partly why the motive for his murder was so hard to find,' said Maisie. 'We assumed that the murderer knew who Ainsley was; but as it turned out, it was the other way round. Thomas Ainsley was killed because he knew who the murderer was — or rather, wasn't.'

'This is ridiculous,' said Edward Mandeville, but he said it without conviction.

'I called on my good friend Mrs Carter recently,' said Maisie. 'She had known Mr Ainsley for many years, and could tell me where he had been in India, whom he had worked with, and when he had visited England. He knew Mr Mandeville senior well, and was on good terms with the family in England. Therefore it follows that he would have known you.' She paused. 'He didn't, did he?'

'Good heavens,' murmured Captain James.

'I doubt that Mr Ainsley said anything outright, but a clever man like you would see the signs, and know what had to be done. Your work depends on being Edward Mandeville for as many years as you can get away with. Your brilliant record and your illustrious name act as a free pass, and anyone who threatens that must be stopped immediately. So that was what you did. You kept Ainsley talking, maybe making occasional slips to keep him interested, and all the time leading him further away from anyone who might help him. Perhaps you admitted that you had a confession, and asked to speak to him privately. And then you cut his throat.'

'You have no proof,' said the man they knew as Edward Mandeville.

'Not as yet,' said Fraser. 'You helpfully gave a false statement that you only spoke to Ainsley for a couple of minutes before he hurried off to meet someone. Therefore we asked potential witnesses the wrong questions. I daresay that if we call them back in, someone will have seen you and Mr Ainsley together long after he was supposed to have left you.'

'But if he isn't Mandeville,' said Captain James, 'then who is he? And where is Edward Mandeville?'

'I'm coming to that,' said Fraser. 'You will be pleased to know, Mandeville, that I tracked down an old colleague who was rather disappointed in you. You had arrived with such a good reputation, and turned out lazy and incurious. You were given less work, which left you free to make mischief, and you were left alone with documents that you should never have seen.' He turned to the viceroy. 'We can guess what happened next. Oh, and they also mentioned your boasting about Rugby School, which I can confirm from my brief time in the secretariat. Edward Mandeville attended Rugby, as did a man named Frank Saunders, another employee of the Indian Civil Service, who sadly died two years ago.'

Mandeville swallowed.

'He recruited you, didn't he?' snapped Fraser. 'Unlike Edward Mandeville, you didn't have wealth and an illustrious name. You had brains and a scholarship education, and after that you would have to make your own way in the world. I doubt Saunders recruited you at Rugby; but he came to find you at Oxford. You would be pleased that an older boy took an interest in you. He no doubt flattered you, indulged your self-pity, and then suggested a way that you could help each other out. Saunders knew he was not strong, and unlikely to survive much longer in India. He wanted to recruit a successor he could trust. And you, with your superficial resemblance to Mandeville and your lack of prospects, were the obvious choice. On a passport you are exactly the same; sandy hair, blue eyes, freckles, above-average height, medium build, no distinguishing marks. The only difference is that moustache you have been cultivating; an excellent screen to hide behind. If you were admitted into the Indian Civil Service, you could replace Edward Mandeville easily. And so you did.'

Anton De Souza sipped his wine, never taking his eyes from Mandeville, and put the glass down with a clink which rang loud in the silent room.

'You made sure that you learned the same languages and chose the same province to start in, and all went well — until sadly, not long before you were due to leave for Bombay, you were killed in an unfortunate accident. You had no close family to mourn you, and you passed from the record. Mandeville was murdered en route to board his ship, and you took his place. Once you were in India, provided you stayed away from Mandeville's father in Calcutta, who else could expose you? You never bargained for Ainsley.'

'And what name will you charge me under, pray?' sneered Mandeville.

'Your own,' Fraser replied. 'I felt you had shamefully neglected your "father", so I paid him a visit. I am afraid that I said I was a friend of yours, and asked him what you were like as a boy. He showed me a photograph of a rugby team, and pointed you out; but it was not you. Then I *did* find you, and Mr Mandeville identified you as "a boy named Higgins". I wired various sources to see what I could learn about you. Joseph Higgins, an orphan, whose education was paid for by a distant uncle to get the boy off his hands. Rugby, then Oxford, then the Indian Civil Service. But your promising career was cut short by a shooting accident. The death certificate for Joseph Higgins records a verdict of death by misadventure, and the person who gave the information is named as Mr Francis Saunders. So Joseph Higgins died, and Edward Mandeville's identity was stolen.'

'Your thoroughness is commendable, Inspector

Hamilton,' said the viceroy. 'Time to call for reinforcements.' He rose to press the bell, and in that instant Higgins leapt up and dashed for the window.

'I told you,' said Captain James, and fired. The bullet hit Higgins in the back of the knee, but he staggered on.

'Don't kill him, James,' said the viceroy calmly. 'I want to keep him alive until we know everything.'

Fraser ran to the window and seized Higgins, who struggled in his grip then threw him off balance. Both men fell onto the rug and rolled this way and that, with neither gaining an advantage.

The door opened and a group of policemen advanced cautiously. 'Which one wants arresting, Your Excellency?' asked the one who appeared to be in charge.

The viceroy rolled his eyes. 'Grab them both, and we'll sort it out afterwards.' His glance fell on Maisie, who was hurrying towards the fighters. 'Miss Frobisher, please stay back. Now is not the time to sew on a button.'

'I think it is,' said Maisie. She watched the pair narrowly, then grabbed Higgins's ankle, pulled down his sock, and drove home a needle threaded with yellow silk. 'That should hold him.'

'What have you done?' cried Higgins.

He twisted round to see; but that movement gave Fraser the advantage, and he pinned Higgins to the ground. 'You may take it from here,' he told the policemen, two of whom moved forward.

'He won't struggle much,' said Maisie. She leaned down to Higgins. 'Just a muscle relaxant. Don't worry, it's only temporary. You'll be fighting fit again when it's time to unburden yourself to the viceroy.'

'Get him out of here,' said Lord Strathcairn. Then he turned to Mr De Souza. 'You have a partial reprieve. Mandeville — Higgins, I mean — is by far a bigger fish to fry; so I shall place you under house arrest till I am ready for you. And when I am, I expect cooperation.' He eyed the two remaining policemen. 'James, take these gentlemen away and explain what is required. Be quick about it, for dinner will be served in twenty minutes.'

Captain James smiled. 'Of course, Your Excellency.' He shot a contemptuous look at Anton De Souza. 'Come quietly, please, sir.'

Once the door had closed behind them, Lord Strathcairn sighed. 'I haven't had an opportunity to thank you both yet,' he said. 'I knew I was being unreasonable in my anger — and Mrs Carter told me so. However, that is not an excuse.' He smiled. 'If you still want to leave my service and return to England, you'll both have to be considerably less useful.' He looked at Maisie. 'I see Mrs Carter has fitted you out. That is a rare honour.'

Maisie could feel her cheeks growing warm. 'I'm just glad that she did,' she said. 'If Higgins had escaped —'

'But he didn't,' said Fraser. 'And he wouldn't. James and I would have seen to that.'

'I know you would,' said the viceroy. 'But would either of you have done it as elegantly as Miss Frobisher?'

'I may be biased, Your Excellency,' said Fraser, 'but in my opinion, no one does anything as elegantly as Miss Frobisher.' He kissed Maisie's hand. 'Although if we ever do marry, I'm not sure I shall let her darn my socks.'

'And if you have any sense,' replied Lord Strathcairn, 'you'll know better than to ask her.' He picked up his glass. 'To you both,' he said, and drank.

CHAPTER 21

'This is an expedition, and no mistake,' said Miss Jeroboam, descending the steps of the veranda.

'Gently,' said Captain James, steadying her. 'No accidents on my watch, if you don't mind.' He looked round. 'Hamilton, would you mind bringing the basket? I seem to have my hands full.'

'And I don't,' murmured Fraser, smiling at Maisie.

'Cheek,' said Maisie. 'Now do your duty and bring the picnic basket.'

Fraser saluted. 'Yes, ma'am.'

They heard a cough, and turned to see Captain James grinning at them. 'When you've quite finished,' he said. 'I'll just get Miss Jeroboam settled.'

Today was Miss Jeroboam's first trip outside Government House since she had arrived. The viceroy's doctor had pronounced her amazingly well, considering, and Miss Jeroboam had begun to talk of Bombay and expeditions.

'Do you think she'll ever go exploring again?' asked Fraser.

Maisie watched Miss Jeroboam, who was looking around with keen interest. 'I hope so,' she said. 'I don't think the viceroy is averse to the idea. And luckily her experience with Mandeville, I mean Higgins, hasn't set her back too much.'

Fraser snorted. 'That's probably the one good thing to come out of this,' he said. 'That villain's admiration helped Miss Jeroboam to take an interest in life again.'

Maisie shivered. 'I'd rather not think about that,' she said. 'He seemed so genuine.'

'I know,' said Fraser. 'I was thoroughly convinced he was a snobbish ass.' He put an arm round Maisie. 'It horrifies me to think that I let you go to that reception with him.'

'You didn't let me,' said Maisie. 'I chose to.' *And what would have happened*, she thought, *if you had carried on being angry and resentful, and that man had continued to seem devoted and nice?*

'I'm sorry I was so — annoyed,' said Fraser. 'I suppose I'm not used to playing second fiddle. As an inspector, one tends not to be. I knew it was necessary, but I didn't like it, and I'm afraid I let my feelings show.' He gazed into her eyes. 'I am truly sorry, Maisie.'

'That's quite all right,' said Maisie, not knowing where to look. 'We had better join the others.'

'I suppose we had,' said Fraser, and took her hand.

'Come along, then.'

But when they arrived under the shady tree, where deckchairs were placed ready and the picnic rug spread, Captain James exclaimed 'I had almost forgotten! The hollow tree over there houses many interesting beetles.'

'Oh, does it?' said Miss Jeroboam. 'Could you show me? I may know some of them.'

'Of course!' Captain James got out of his deckchair and offered Miss Jeroboam a hand. 'Shall we?' He led her away rather quickly. 'Back in a few minutes,' he called. 'I'm sure you two can amuse yourselves.'

'He's in a funny mood,' said Maisie, sitting down. She opened the basket and began to arrange plates and tumblers. 'Lemonade?'

'Yes please,' said Fraser. 'Have you heard from your family lately?'

Maisie giggled. 'I have. Mother said in her last letter that India must be shockingly dull, since I seem to have nothing to write about.' She smiled at Fraser. 'Can you imagine if I told her what I've been doing?'

'I'd rather not,' said Fraser. 'You could tell her that you have taken up sewing.'

'I could,' said Maisie, 'for Mrs Carter has made me a present of a darning mushroom. And no, you really don't want to know.'

'At this rate you will be even more fearsome than you already are,' Fraser said lightly.

'I'm not fearsome!' cried Maisie. 'I'm very nice when you get to know me.'

Fraser smirked. 'I'm not sure Higgins would agree.'

'Will you leave that man out of this?' said Maisie. 'We are supposed to be having a holiday and not thinking of work at all.'

'You're absolutely right,' said Fraser. 'My family are sticklers for tradition. Are yours?'

'Not particularly,' said Maisie. 'They were happy for me to move out and live in my own house, and I don't think they mind too much that I have not got married and produced an heir yet.'

Fraser drew his deckchair a little closer. 'About that,' he murmured. 'I never quite asked you, did I? Not properly, on one knee in the dirt, like you wanted.'

Captain James, standing beside an elderly tree, seemed to be talking earnestly to Miss Jeroboam. He caught Maisie's eye, then moved Miss Jeroboam so that they both faced away. Maisie frowned. 'No, you —' She turned to find Fraser on one knee.

'I could have lost you,' he said. 'I'm not risking that again. If a pair of ruined trousers is the price I must pay, then I'm willing. Marry me, Maisie. Please.' He rummaged in his pocket and brought out a small box. 'It isn't what I had in mind, but perhaps it will do for now.' He opened the box, and a large diamond winked at Maisie. 'If you don't like it we can reset it, or find something else, or —'

'Do be quiet,' cried Maisie, dropping to her knees before him, heedless of her white dress. 'Yes, Fraser, yes!' She threw her arms round him with such vigour that he almost fell backwards.

'That's definitely a yes, then?' he asked, with a broad

grin.

'How many times do you want me to say it?' Maisie wiped away a tear which had appeared from nowhere.

'As many times as you like, Maisie.' Fraser took her hand and slid the ring on her finger. 'If it doesn't fit, we can alter it —'

'It's perfect.' Maisie held her hand to the light and watched the diamond twinkle with secret rainbows. 'I can probably send heliographs with it if I'm ever in a tight spot.'

'I'd say that I hope that won't ever happen,' said Fraser. 'But with you, it probably will.'

'Hmm,' said Maisie. 'Whom did I rescue with my sewing kit the other day?'

'I was winning,' said Fraser. 'It was only a matter of time.'

'Men!' proclaimed Maisie, with her nose in the air.

'Since you're so capable, you may give me a hand up,' said Fraser. 'I have demonstrated my devotion for quite long enough.'

'That you have,' said Maisie, getting to her feet and extending a hand. 'I wouldn't want it to run out.' She glanced towards the tree, where Captain James and Miss Jeroboam were still talking. 'I suppose it will be a long engagement.'

'That was one of the reasons why I hesitated,' said Fraser. 'I didn't think you would be too offended that I hadn't asked your father's permission first —'

Maisie snorted. 'I should hope not.'

'If I may continue,' said Fraser. 'But I thought you'd

like them to be at your wedding.'

'Of course I would,' said Maisie. 'And my friends.' Captain James was gesticulating at the top of the tree. 'Although it would be romantic to elope.'

'Would it, now.' Fraser laughed. 'We are a long way from Gretna Green.'

'Maisie Hamilton,' Maisie said thoughtfully. 'It has rather a ring to it.'

'It does,' said Fraser. He leaned across and kissed her. 'Will you be terribly sorry to lose the Frobisher?'

Maisie considered. 'I'm used to it, but not particularly attached.'

'That's good,' said Fraser. 'I thought with your father, and the explorer —'

Maisie stared at him. 'What explorer?'

Fraser stared back. 'Did your governesses and masters teach you nothing, Maisie Frobisher?'

'Nothing useful,' said Maisie. 'Most of my education came from my father's library.'

'Martin Frobisher,' said Fraser. 'Sixteenth-century explorer and privateer. He sailed all over the place and helped to repel the Spanish Armada.' He smiled. 'Perhaps he is a distant relative of yours; a many-greats grandfather.'

Captain James and Miss Jeroboam were returning. As they grew closer Maisie could see an enquiring expression on Captain James's face, which was quickly replaced by a grin. *Once he knows, everybody will know*, she thought. *I must wire Mother tonight. Not to mention Connie.* She imagined the electrical telegraph sparking her message across the world, completing in seconds a journey which would have taken Martin Frobisher many years. *Yet I have discovered new things too*, she thought. *A bigger world, full of adventure and intrigue, and evil, and good.* She blinked. *And when we marry, we must make sure we never lose it.*

'You look very thoughtful,' said Fraser. 'Are you thinking of your ancestor?'

Maisie smiled. 'Yes, I am.' She thought of the ships and trains and rickshaws that had carried her to where she was now, sitting in the Viceroy of India's garden with her fiancé. 'Travelling must run in the family.'

ACKNOWLEDGEMENTS

As usual, my first thanks are for my beta readers — Carol Bissett, Ruth Cunliffe, Paula Harmon and Stephen Lenhardt, who read the manuscript in double-quick time, and made several insightful observations. The book wouldn't be the same without you.

My next thanks are to John Croall, who proofread the book for me. This time his specialist subject was music! Any errors which remain are of course my responsibility.

A big second thank you to my husband Stephen Lenhardt — he not only reads what I write (I assume he enjoys it), but has to put up with me during the process. At least for this book I spent all the drafting time outside — which now, writing this sentence in March 2020, in partial lockdown, seems almost unbelievable.

As in the previous two books, I've used the place names that were current at the time, e.g. Bombay instead of Mumbai, Calcutta instead of Kolkata.

And finally, thanks to you, my reader! I hope you've enjoyed Maisie's third adventure, and if you could leave a short review or a star rating for *Gone To Ground* on Amazon or Goodreads, I'd appreciate it very much.

Font and image credits

Fonts:

Title font: Limelight by Eben Sorkin: https://www.fontsquirrel.com/fonts/limelight. License — SIL Open Font License v.1.10: http://scripts.sil.org/OFL

Script font: Alex Brush by TypeSETit: https://www.fontsquirrel.com/fonts/alex-brush. License — SIL Open Font License v.1.10: http://scripts.sil.org/OFL

Graphics:

Forest background: Forest scene at daytime and night time free vector, created by brgfx: https://www.freepik.com/free-vector/forest-scene-daytime-nighttime_4932757.htm

Cloaked figure: Realistic set of red cloaks with hoods isolated on white background, created by vectorpocket: https://www.freepik.com/free-vector/realistic-set-red-cloaks-with-hoods-isolated-white-background_3264745.htm

Leopard: Leopard Walking (reversed and edited to put him behind the tree): Illustration 42892915 © Ievgen Melamud: dreamstime.com: https://www.dreamstime.com/

stock-illustration-leopard-walking-wild-big-cat-realistic-illustration-image42892915

Series frame: frame vector created by alvaro_cabrera: https://www.freepik.com/free-vector/eight-ornamental-frames_961366.htm

Maisie cameo (modified and recoloured): Vintage vector created by freepik: https://www.freepik.com/free-vector/beautiful-woman-silhouette_811219.htm

Leopard chapter vignette: Leopard silhouette created by Viviana at clker.com

Cover created using GIMP image editor: www.gimp.org.

ABOUT LIZ HEDGECOCK

Liz Hedgecock grew up in London, England, did an English degree, and then took forever to start writing. After several years working in the National Health Service, some short stories crept into the world. A few even won prizes. Then the stories started to grow longer…

Now Liz travels between the nineteenth and twenty-first centuries, murdering people. To be fair, she does usually clean up after herself.

Liz's reimaginings of Sherlock Holmes, her Pippa Parker cozy mystery series, and the Caster & Fleet Victorian mystery series (written with Paula Harmon), are available in ebook and paperback.

Liz lives in Cheshire with her husband and two sons, and when she's not writing or child-wrangling you can usually find her reading, messing about on Twitter, or cooing over stuff in museums and art galleries. That's her story, anyway, and she's sticking to it.

Website/blog: http://lizhedgecock.wordpress.com
Facebook: http://www.facebook.com/lizhedgecockwrites
Twitter: http://twitter.com/lizhedgecock
Goodreads: https://www.goodreads.com/lizhedgecock

BOOKS BY LIZ HEDGECOCK

Short stories
The Secret Notebook of Sherlock Holmes
Bitesize
The Adventure of the Scarlet Rosebud

Halloween Sherlock series (novelettes)
The Case of the Snow-White Lady
Sherlock Holmes and the Deathly Fog
The Case of the Curious Cabinet

Sherlock & Jack series (novellas)
A Jar Of Thursday
Something Blue
A Phoenix Rises

Mrs Hudson & Sherlock Holmes series (novels)
A House Of Mirrors
In Sherlock's Shadow

Pippa Parker Mysteries (novels)
Murder At The Playgroup
Murder In The Choir
A Fete Worse Than Death
Murder in the Meadow
The QWERTY Murders

Caster & Fleet Mysteries (with Paula Harmon)
The Case of the Black Tulips

The Case of the Runaway Client
The Case of the Deceased Clerk
The Case of the Masquerade Mob
The Case of the Fateful Legacy
The Case of the Crystal Kisses

Maisie Frobisher Mysteries (novels)
All At Sea
Off The Map
Gone To Ground

For children (with Zoe Harmon)
A Christmas Carrot

WHITE RHINO BOOKS

Printed in Great Britain
by Amazon